"I don't, for a second, see you as a believer in fate."

"Really?" Roth answered.

His eyes were riveting. Hannah couldn't think or move. A strange combination of fear and anticipation began to sizzle along her nerves.

"Assumptions, Miss Hudson, can be dangerous," he murmured. "You hardly know me."

His hand suddenly cupped the back of her head, drawing her face to his. Hungry, searching lips covered hers. The boldness of his act sung through her veins, his kiss more potent and delicious than she dared admit. Her arms snaking around his shoulders, she leaned in, breast to chest, her body's response an explicit "yes."

As surprisingly as it began, his kiss ended. Roth's fingers trailed slowly, deliberately downward, pausing at her nape. "You're right about one thing," he whispered. "I don't believe in fate." Cunning fingers drifted languidly on, southward along her spine, until his hand came to rest provocatively, just below the small of her back. "But, I love a challenge."

BLUE MOON BRIDE

Renee Roszel

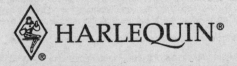

TORONTO • NEW YORK • LONDON
AMSTERDAM • PARIS • SYDNEY • HAMBURG
STOCKHOLM • ATHENS • TOKYO • MILAN • MADRID
PRAGUE • WARSAW • BUDAPEST • AUCKLAND

ISBN 0-373-03898-4

BLUE MOON BRIDE

First North American Publication 2006.

Copyright © 2006 by Renee Roszel Wilson.

This edition published by arrangement with Harlequin Books S.A.

Renee Roszel has been writing romances for over two decades and finds it hard to believe she's had such a dream career for so long. Over the years she's traveled to far-flung, exotic places such as the USSR (before the breakup) and to Germany's East Berlin (before the wall tumbled). She has toured her native America, too, scuba diving in Hawaii, the Cayman Islands and Florida Keys. Her grown sons live in Illinois and Florida, making for farther fun vacation visits. At present, she and her husband have just finished building their own home on Grand Lake in northeastern Oklahoma, where Renee looks forward to continuing her writing, inspired by the tranquility and native beauty of one of Oklahoma's most celebrated waterways.

Renee loves to hear from her readers. Visit her Web site at www.ReneeRoszel.com

Books by Renee Roszel

HARLEQUIN ROMANCE®
3752—SURRENDER TO A PLAYBOY
3778—A BRIDE FOR THE HOLIDAYS
3865—JUST FRIENDS TO...JUST MARRIED

To Linda Fildew
My Editor, My Friend

CHAPTER ONE

HANNAH found herself smiling for the first time in weeks. She gazed up at the moon. It hung in the night sky, centered in an arched window of the last standing wall amid the ruins of an old stone church. From her perch on a granite garden bench, Hannah stared, transfixed, at the glowing orb so improbably framed in the vaulted opening that once housed stained glass.

The spectacle was even more unique because it was the second full moon this month. "A blue moon," she whispered, wondering how many others had witnessed the awe inspiring sight from this enchanting perspective. Her tentative smile lingered. She was glad that the proprietress of the inn suggested she come out here. The wildflower garden emanated quiet and peace, the perfectly framed moon adding a touch of magic. For the moment her troubles receded enough to allow her to feel briefly uplifted. Or at least not completely demoralized, as she had since quitting her job a month ago.

She sighed, unsettled by the profound gloom she heard in her tone. But how else should she feel after discovering she was a water cooler joke?

How could she have let Milo Brisco turn her into his puppet? Caught up in her mindless infatuation for the smooth-talking lawyer, she had let him convince her to bleach her perfectly respectable dark blond hair to "Marilyn Monroe platinum," and change the natural, curly way she wore it into a sleek, extreme style that took an hour to achieve every morning. Not to mention how he had persuaded her to forgo her moderate office attire and allow *him* to choose trendy, hip, patently sexy, clothes.

She experienced a surge of self-condemnation. How could she have been so blinded by her weakness for the man to allow him to manipulate her? She thought she had more backbone than that. Obviously she was wrong.

Two years ago, after her parents' divorce, she committed herself to being an independent woman, hanging on to no man for survival or fulfillment. Her parents' ugly split taught her that much: no man's midlife crisis and panting search for a trophy wife would devastate her as it had her mother. Dorothy Hudson was left alone, depressed, reduced to eking out a living as a burger joint cook.

On the other side of that coin, neither did she intend to become a clingy, passive nincompoop like Cindy, her philandering father's latest trophy gal-pal, barely twenty. The empty-headed twit was *six* years younger than Hannah.

Determined never to become a "Dorothy" or a "Cindy" she had redoubled her efforts at building a solid career. Then, four months ago, she fell hard for Milo Brisco. "The egomaniac jerk," she mumbled.

The first blow came suddenly and rudely when she overheard him bragging around the office about his "ingenious" transformation of her. She covered her ears wishing she could erase the sound of his voice, but knowing she would never drown out the memory of his crowing, or the sneer in his tone when he boasted, "Roth and I had a good laugh about how I turned a mediocre middle manager into serious arm candy!"

Arm candy! She cringed. Were two more brutally sexist words ever uttered by a man?

That was bad enough, but the second, and much worse blow,

had been the one, foul word, *mediocre*. That mean-spirited description broke her heart every time she thought about it. Hannah had worked hard at her job. She thought she more than earned her salary. Managing the finance department wasn't flashy or earth shaking, but even with the day-to-day tussles she had with her subordinates, dealing with their personality quirks, screwups and petty jealousies, she ran a pretty smooth department. At least she'd thought so.

Then to hear herself belittled by a man who supposedly cared for her? She felt shamed and betrayed. She knew she could have lived down an office affair and the "arm candy" swipe, but mediocre? For nearly five years she'd done the best job she knew how for Jerric Oil, so clearly hard work and doing her best weren't enough.

"And Roth laughed!" she muttered. Roth Jerric *laughed*. She'd found the charismatic company president and founder attractive, and had a great deal of respect for him. Misplaced, as it turned out. He thought of her as mediocre!

Enduring a grisly sleepless night after being humiliated and insulted, she realized trying to prove herself "*not* mediocre" would be a fool's errand. After all, she'd done her best. Evidently her best had been laughable to the company president. Consequently, disillusioned, her self-confidence wrecked, the next morning she resigned.

So now, with her savings dwindling, she needed a job. But more than that she needed to prove to herself that she was not mediocre. How did a person do that? What if she really was mediocre and never would be better than "average"?

No! she told herself. *Hannah Hudson you are not mediocre.* Sure, she'd made a fool of herself over Milo. That mistake was easy enough to fix with dark blond hair dye and a donation of flashy clothes to charity. But the mediocre label dogged her, hurt her. How did she disprove that? She wasn't sure, but she planned to do it or die trying.

"I'll show you, Milo," she muttered. "You, too, Roth Jerric!"

"Excuse me?"

The male voice intruding on Hannah's reverie brought her head up with a jerk. A moment of disorientation scattered her wits before she realized the voice had come from behind her, the general vicinity of the garden's stone path. With self-protective dispatch, she scooted around to face whoever had spoken. Her brain was on the verge of issuing the *"stand up"* command when a man came into focus, brightly illuminated in the moonlight. Witnessing his starkly lit features short-circuited the command to stand, and she froze where she sat.

Not him!

She recognized the sharp angles of his face. Those strong, rough-cut features had always held a masculine, sensual attraction for her, but in such naked illumination the effect of light and shadow transformed mere handsome into a stunning picture of symmetry and strength. Her breath caught painfully.

She knew those eyes, too. They appeared dark and bottomless in the false light, but she knew them to be sky-blue and compelling. She also recognized the assertive set of his shoulders and the way his raven-black hair tapered concisely to his collar. What she didn't know was why fate decided to play this cruel trick on her.

Why was Roth Jerric, of all people, eavesdropping on her most private thoughts—just when she'd spoken his name, now repugnant to her? It took a few seconds to find her voice. When she did, she blurted, "What are *you* doing here?"

He appeared surprised by the edge in her question. Apparently he was unaccustomed to being *persona non grata*. "Walking," he said, his brow crinkling in a slight frown.

His looming presence, aglow with reflected moonlight, gave him a godlike aura. Maybe it was because he was so tall, or because he wore a white dress shirt and light trousers, but the effect was disquieting. She could feel her pulse rate jump. That annoyed her. Why must her body react so strongly to a man who dismissed her with a laugh. Emotionally unraveled, her confidence damaged, she didn't need this—this ultrasuccessful, ultradominant—SOB around.

Her stress and frustration mutated into anger. "I came out here to be alone. To think." That wasn't totally true. She came out here to be alone, true. But she didn't want to think. She wanted to blank out completely. Just breathe deeply and try to find a little calm.

"So did I," he said. "I didn't see you."

"Strange. I'm lit up like a firecracker."

His brow crinkled further. "If I bruised your ego for not noticing you, miss, I apologize. I was lost in thought."

"My ego isn't the point." He'd called her "miss." Why? He knew her well enough to laugh at her! Provoked, she pushed up to stand. "Pretending you don't know me is insulting."

He appeared troubled. She couldn't decide if the expression was residue from whatever he'd been thinking about, or if he was having trouble maintaining the fiction that he didn't know precisely who she was. "Have we met before?" She watched him as he scanned her face. "You do look familiar."

She crossed her arms. "I should. I worked for you for nearly five years, the last six months as your finance manager." *According to you, your mediocre finance manager,* she added mentally, swallowing hard. She wished she could throw his insult back at him, but she couldn't bring herself to, couldn't bear to hear it out loud again. Close to tears, she fought to keep her lips from trembling.

His eyebrows dipped in apparent concentration.

She wasn't sure if she was more disconcerted that he didn't appear to remember her than if he'd slapped his thigh, chortling, *"Oh, right, right, right—you're the mediocre manager and Milo's arm candy!"*

"I'm the arm candy." She flinched. How could she have said *that* out loud? She'd meant to say her name.

His reaction, at first, was no reaction at all. After a second when he blinked and squinted at her, she knew he knew. "The arm...?" He paused for a heartbeat, then added, "Oh."

That quietly spoken "oh" had the impact of a ton of bricks falling on her. She felt sick, especially now that she sensed he hadn't recognized her. She didn't look much like she had the last time he saw her. Her severe platinum hairstyle was gone, transformed to its original dark blond, curly, shoulder-length style. Plus she wore jeans and an oversize T-shirt rather than the body-hugging, sexy-sophisticated attire of Milo's choosing.

Darn her impulsive nature. She could have made it through this detestable encounter without him recalling her, if she'd only engaged her brain before her mouth.

Sadly the damage was done, so she might as well salvage what she could of her pride. Straightening her shoulders, she clasped her hands before her, working to appear strong and as little like arm candy as possible. "My name is Hannah Hudson, until recently your finance department manager. I resigned at the end of May."

He inclined his head slightly, appearing to absorb that as he scanned her face again. "Of course. Miss Hudson." He said her name without a hint of a snicker or sneer. "I remember you now. Since your promotion we've been in several meetings together."

"Once or twice," she corrected. "Usually your VP of finance presided."

"You look different," he said.

"Yeah, well, I've joined the ACA." His puzzled expression didn't surprise her.

"The what?" he asked.

"It's 'Arm Candy Anonymous.'"

He smiled as though finding her sarcasm clever, "Forgive me for not recognizing you." He held out a hand, long-fingered and steady. She experienced a tremor of hesitation. Did he expect her to take it? Besides having a reputation for enjoying plenty of arm candy himself, and for being married to his work, he was known for his diplomacy. "To be fair, I was at a disadvantage. Your face is in shadow."

He had a point—about her face being in shadow—but she ignored it, just as she ignored his outstretched hand. "You're not staying here, are you?" She prayed for his response to be no. When she won her free two-week stay at the quaint inn on Grand Lake in Northeastern Oklahoma, she'd been euphoric. She needed distance from Jerric Oil and Oklahoma City, not to mention precious time to heal, to recover her self-confidence. She planned to use this trip to reevaluate where she was going and what she wanted to do with her future. Having anybody at the inn aware of her poisoned reputation at Jerric Oil would put a huge damper on her recovery—most particularly if that somebody's name was *Jerric*.

"I'm a guest here." His grin grew crooked and wry. "You know, Miss Hudson," he went on, "questions like that can be hard on a man's ego."

"For how long?"

"How long will my ego suffer?"

Was he trying to make her crazy? "No! What is it with you and egos?" She licked her lips, nervous. "I'm asking how long you'll be here?"

"A couple of weeks."

Horrible news. The worst possible news. Not that she was hard on his ego. It could use some filing down. The horrible news was that he would be a guest at the inn as long as she. "Oh, no. That's how long I'll be here."

"Ouch," he said with a exaggerated cringe.

"Sucks, doesn't it," she grumbled, "discovering somebody doesn't find you all that terrific." She experienced a rush of vindication. "Try seeing it from my perspective," she said. "I'm sure you can understand why I might be upset that you're here."

"Not really." His response held a note of impatience, as

though her continued digs were taking a toll on his ability to remain diplomatic.

That was too bad. "I'm here to get away from—from everything that reminds me of—of…" She shrugged, arms outstretched. "You know."

"Not really," he repeated.

"Oh, please." She spun away. "You know why I had to leave Jerric Oil."

"I assume you got a better offer."

"That's what you *assume?*" she asked, sarcasm edging her tone. "Well, you assume *wrong.*"

He said nothing for a moment. The warm, June breeze ruffled the flowers. They rustled in the darkness, seeming to gossip in whispers. "Then why—"

"Don't you dare ask me why I left!" she cut in. *Talk about nerve!* She plunked down on the stone bench, grimacing at the pain in her backside.

"But you seem upset, and I—"

"You *think?*" she demanded. "If you don't mind, I'm not in the mood to chat."

The night breeze rustled the flowers again. They bobbed and nodded, giving rise to more stage whispers. After a stressful few seconds, Roth Jerric cleared his throat. "If you'll excuse me then?"

She clamped her fingers over the edge of the bench and stared straight ahead, looking at nothing. If she didn't respond, he'd get the idea, even if he was as dense as the granite she sat on.

"It was fascinating visiting with you, Miss Hudson," he said, his remark clearly cynical. She wanted to smart-off but managed to keep her mouth shut. It didn't give her any satisfaction, but she wanted him to leave, and that wouldn't happen if she kept their exchange going.

She began a calming count to ten. One…two…three… "Okay!" She spun around. "Just so you get it, I am *no* man's arm candy, and hearing Milo smirking around the office, objectifying me that way, and knowing—*others*—agreed…" She wanted to say, *You for instance*. So unstrung with doubt about her ability, she couldn't bring herself to acknowledge the rest. She went on with what she could admit. "Naturally I couldn't stay at Jerric Oil after that." Too late, she wished she hadn't revealed that much. She bit her tongue for its betrayal.

Roth had begun to move toward the inn, but stopped with her outburst. For an instant he appeared startled, then he chuckled deep in his throat.

Laughing?

At her!

Again!

Okay, if he wanted war, he could have war. "You have a warped sense of humor, Mr. Jerric!"

He shook his head. "You've got to be kidding."

Had she heard him right? "Kidding?"

"Yes, kidding." He looked dubious, and vaguely amused.

Amused! She burned with resentment. "Not at all!" She knew her cheeks blazed bright red and was grateful for the darkness. Feeling feisty, she shot to her feet. "Obviously you find my humiliation a total hoot."

He started to speak, but she threw up a halting hand. "*Don't.* Your judgments don't interest me. Just go."

She could tell by the play of shadow and light across his jaw he clenched his teeth. After a drawn-out silence, he nodded curtly, broke eye contact and strode off along the stone path.

She watched his exodus until she realized what she was doing, then she turned away. After a few minutes, she managed to calm down. She lifted her gaze toward the vaulted window in the old, stone wall. The moon no longer hung dead center in the space, but was set off-kilter in a corner. She felt as askew as it looked.

Unbidden, her attention slid back to the inn. In the distance she could see the ghostly image of Roth Jerric disappearing around the corner toward the front porch. She closed her eyes. Struggling to compose herself she sucked in a breath of fresh, night air.

"Okay, Hannah," she whispered. "For the sake of your healing, keep your distance from…" She faltered on the words, so she went on silently…*from that smug, disturbing SOB, Roth Jerric.*

Roth walked away from Hannah feeling like crap. Of course, he already felt that way when he began his walk, but his brief encounter with the woman on the bench left him not only annoyed but confused. He didn't need a fortune teller to see that she hated him, but he couldn't imagine why. He'd spoken to her at meetings on occasion, or nodded a casual hello in the elevator from time to time. But he'd never said anything to upset her, let alone cause her to resign.

And he certainly hadn't been laughing at her out there. He'd simply been incredulous that she would quit her job over anything Milo had said. The man was a competent lawyer, but on a personal level Roth found him to be a blowhard and a braggart. Had Miss Hudson given him half a chance he would have said so. Clearly his opinion was as unwelcome as his presence.

"Let it go, Jerric," he muttered. "You have problems of your own." He bounded up the steps to the inn's expansive front porch and walked across the wooden planking toward the screen door. It was a different screen door from the one he remembered from his youth, when this house had been his family home. But it had the same rusty screech when pulled open.

The scarred oak door was the same one from all those years ago. He recognized it, even painted white instead of the bright green he remembered. He paused, his hand on the brass doorknob, its oval shape familiar in his grasp. It seemed smaller than it had when he lived there. He supposed it should, since he was ten when his family moved from this house, originally the parsonage for the old church which had burned down in 1919.

The house was a century old, but well-built. It had gone through many incarnations since the demise of the countryside church. When Roth lived there the property was their chicken farm. After his father died, his mother moved him and his older sister, Grace, to Oklahoma's state capital, where she worked as a secretary. He'd never returned to his childhood home until today, when he made the sudden decision to get away from the rat race, seek out his roots. He could no longer avoid dealing with an inner struggle growing inside him, gnawing, eating away at his soul.

He was disillusioned with the conflict between his aspirations and the reality of his life. However successful he appeared on the surface, he was not a happy man. The disillusionment began with his disappointing marriage and the death of his month-old son, Colin. Not long after the infant's death, his teetering marriage collapsed. That was six years ago. Since then, he had closed off emotionally, throwing himself into work.

He supposed, to his colleagues, he seemed like a golden boy, enviable for his wealth and swank bachelor lifestyle. But in truth, he was in crisis. So, in a moment of nostalgic weakness, he'd sought out his family home, now the Blue Moon Inn. He hoped to recapture a time he remembered fondly, before life became a succession of tough negotiations, 24/7 business stress, bitter disillusionment and gut-wrenching loss.

He leaned against the door, tired all the way to his bones. As far back as he could remember, he got everything he went after. Yet whether his fault or not, he had lost what had been most dear to him—his wife and son. Everything else he had, money, power and success, seemed pale and flat by comparison.

He'd come to the Blue Moon Inn to get back his boyhood exuberance, and that's what he planned to do. He straightened and sucked in a deep breath. Enough of this maudlin self-pity. He twisted the knob and strode inside.

The inn's brightly lit foyer brought into sharp focus the worn wood floors and moldings, faded oriental rugs and dark oil paintings in need of cleaning. There were other art pieces tacked to walls. Newer works. Some exhibited talent. Others, in his opinion, ran more to smeared and spattered monstrosities.

The Blue Moon Inn wasn't the sort of deluxe retreat he was accustomed to, but he hadn't come for a luxurious vacation or a romantic getaway with a finicky girlfriend. This was the home of his heart, before it had been broken, then put to sleep as a safeguard against pain. He didn't know if what he hoped for was possible, but he planned to spend these two weeks finding a way to repair his crumbling *joie de vivre*.

"Why, hello there, Mr., uh," came a warbly female voice he recognized as that of his hostess.

He turned toward the sound of her shuffling approach. "Jerric," he helped. "Roth Jerric."

The pear-shaped, elderly woman crossed the parlor in his direction. Close behind her trailed a wire-haired, gray mongrel the size of a large cat. "Of course," she said. "I thought you'd gone to bed." The parlor from which his hostess exited was lit by one lamp, its shade yellowed with age. That lone lamp spilled jaundiced light across outdated, faded furnishings. Plainly the Blue Moon Inn had seen better days.

Out of years of habit, Roth pasted on a casual grin. "Hello, Mrs. Peterson." He glanced at his wristwatch. Nearly midnight. "You're up late."

"Oh, there's much to be done, Mr. Johnson."

"Jerric," he corrected.

"Yes, yes, certainly," she said, sounding a bit preoccupied. Barely five feet tall, she wore a green shirtdress and crisp, white apron. She wasn't smiling. "You were outside?"

He nodded. "Is something wrong?"

"I don't know. Did you happen to see a woman out there? In the garden in the church ruins, perhaps?"

"Yes. Were you looking for her?" He felt something brush his leg and looked down to see the mutt, sniffing him. He shifted away. The dog seemed to get the hint, or lost interest, because it returned to stand beside the woman, its feet making light tapping sounds on the scarred oak.

"I sent her out there. I mean…" Mrs. Peterson's worry-creased expression didn't ease. "You didn't go near her, did you?"

What an odd query. "Actually, yes. We spoke for a moment."

"Oh, gracious!" The woman clasped both hands to her breast. "Are you saying you stood by *that* bench in the—the *moonlight?* With *her?*"

He nodded, bewildered by the alarm in the woman's question.

"Oh, *no!*" she cried, startling the dog. It barked, the sound high-pitched and curiously reminiscent of its elderly owner. "Hush, Miss Mischief," she admonished, not looking at the animal. She ran both hands through short-cropped, iron-colored hair. "All my work, my planning, ruined."

He clenched his teeth. What in Hades was going on? He'd been at the inn for less than two hours, done nothing but unpack and take a blasted walk, and already two women were upset with him. "Your friend in the garden wasn't thrilled about my being there, either," he said. "Would you mind explaining what was so wrong with my speaking to her?"

"Wrong?" the woman echoed, her tone forlorn. "Everything!" Her plump cheeks pinkened with indignation. "Now you…" She glanced in the direction of the garden. "And she…oh, it's all gone so badly." She pulled a rumpled handkerchief from her apron pocket and pressed it to her lips.

"What's gone badly?" he asked.

She swiped at her nose then pushed the kerchief back into her apron pocket. As she lifted her gaze to meet his, she looked as though she was trying to recapture her poise. "I'm sorry for my behavior, Mr. Johnson."

"It's Jerric," he said, beginning to wonder if the woman would ever get his name right. "Roth Jerric."

"Yes, yes." She nodded. Looking distracted, she patted her hair, still not quite reclaiming her "hostess" aplomb. "Forgive me. I'm an old lady who had a lovely flight of fancy—a hope you might say—to enhance two deserving young people's lives. And—well—because of you, all my effort has been smashed on the rocks of mischance." She attempted a smile. "It wasn't your fault. You didn't know."

"Didn't know what?" he asked. Good Lord, he'd somehow smashed this woman's hopes for something important enough to drive her to the brink of tears. How was that possible simply by speaking with Hannah Hudson? The experience hadn't been any great thrill for him, that was certain.

"You didn't know—about the blue moon, and about…" She shook her head. Her eyes, a faded dust-brown behind wire-rimmed spectacles, expressed a mournfulness she couldn't mask with apologetic murmurings. "I trust you found her delightful," she said.

That remark surprised him. He thought about saying, though he found her attractive, her disposition left a great deal to be desired. Instead he asked, "Why?"

"Because you must," she said sadly. "Fate has spoken, dear boy."

He had no idea what she meant and started to ask, but she wasn't through speaking.

"When the sheriff comes, would you mind telling him he's too late?"

"Sheriff?" He felt like he'd stepped into the twilight zone. Fate? Sheriff? "Too late for what?"

"For them." She made a weak effort at a pleasant expression. "He should have been here an hour ago. When he comes, ask him why he was late. Deacon Vance is his name. A darling man. Widower, you know, and only thirty-five." She turned away, heaving a ragged sigh. "So sad. But who am I to question Madam Fate?" Her back to Roth, she shuffled off down a dimly lit hallway toward the back of the house. "Come along, Missy Mis," she said unnecessarily, since the dog trailed close behind her. "Good night, Mr. Johnson."

He started to correct her mistake but decided it didn't matter. Other problems loomed larger. Had he heard her right? She'd spoken more to herself than to him. What had she said about questioning Madam Fate? And the sheriff was too late? For what? And what had he ruined by simply speaking to the stormy Miss Hudson?

"What in Hades just happened here?" he muttered.

After a moment a distant door slammed. Apparently his hostess was now ensconced in her quarters.

A bell pealed nearby, jarring him. He shook his head at himself. It was only a damn phone. Clearly his nerves were shot, and so far his stay at the inn hadn't helped his mental state. Facing the fact that he'd been put in charge, he walked to the reservation desk, outfitted in what was once a hallway closet. He grabbed the receiver. "Jerric here."

"What?" the male voice on the other end of the line asked.

Roth felt like an idiot. "I mean, Blue Moon Inn."

"Who is this?"

Roth didn't enjoy this kind of phone call. "Who is this?" he asked.

"This is Sheriff Deacon Vance. I ask again, who is this?"

"Oh, Sheriff. This is Roth Jerric, a guest at the inn. Mrs. Peterson went to bed. She asked me to tell you you're too late. I'm guessing you don't need to come out."

"Too late?"

Roth was relieved to hear the sheriff's confusion. "That's what she said, along with other things—something about

Madam Fate and hopes crashing on rocks. To tell the truth…"
He had a thought that seemed worth exploring. "Does the
woman have a drinking problem?"

Hearty laughter exploded on the other end of the line. "What
she has is a meddling problem. Tell me, Jerric, is a young,
attractive female staying at the inn?"

He thought about Hannah Hudson, her lithe, slender frame
and free-falling blond hair. He recalled stunning, gray-green
eyes and remembered the first time he noticed them. He and
Hannah happened to be on the same elevator when their glances
chanced to meet. He was so struck by the rare beauty of those
eyes he'd lost his train of thought. That never happened to him,
so the moment stuck in his mind. And her smile. He recalled
that, too—singularly sweet. Every time he saw it he had the
feeling it reached clear to her soul.

Tonight she hadn't smiled. Quite the contrary. But to answer
the sheriff's question, she was damn attractive, even with the
attitude. "Yes, there's an attractive woman staying here."

"Ah-ha."

"What does that mean?"

"It means, Joan Peterson is up to her matchmaking tricks,"
he said. "She called me insisting a prowler was roaming the
grounds. Wanted me there pronto. On the way I got side-
tracked rescuing a teenage couple from their overturned
pickup. When will young lovers learn that French kissing
while traveling sixty miles an hour on a country road isn't
very bright? They were lucky they wore their seat belts and
the streambed they ended up in wasn't deep." There was silence on the line for a few seconds. "Look, apologize to her
for me," he said. "Tell her duty called and I'm sorry about the
blue moon."

"Right." Roth didn't quite catch the last thing Deacon said.
"What about a blue—"

Too late. The sheriff had hung up. What did he mean he was

sorry about the blue moon? "Is everybody crazy around here?" he asked the empty lobby.

Turning away from the registration desk, he stared down the hallway where he had last seen Joan Peterson. At a loss, he began to get angry. He'd come to the blasted inn hoping to conjure up a new burst of optimism and clarity. So far all he'd managed to conjure up was a bucket load of female outrage.

CHAPTER TWO

HANNAH'S vow to keep her distance from the annoying Roth Jerric wasn't as easy to keep as she hoped, considering they shared a bathroom. That afternoon when she arrived, the idea of sharing it with strangers hadn't seemed alarming. She'd pictured some sweet elderly couple that would retire early, or newlyweds oblivious to anyone but each other, or some health nut who would hike or canoe all day.

In her worst nightmare she never imagined her bath-mate would be her belittling ex-boss, or so—well, so conspicuously *male*. Her problems began when she returned from her midnight sojourn in the garden, worn-out and ready for a long soak in the tub. When she started to open the door, she heard the shower running. Darn the man. Why couldn't he have showered in the hour he had once he left her alone?

Though she preferred to think she and Roth had nothing in common, by the next morning things were shaping up to appear that they shared an identical sleeping, waking and hygiene schedule.

She had just gone into the bathroom when she heard a knock. Being close to the booming sound, she jumped and gasped. Never in her life had the simple act of taking a bath caused her so much anxiety. She stood there naked, her nerves raw, one step away from climbing into the ancient clawfoot tub. "What?" she asked, stress ripe in her tone.

"Are you about done?"

"No," she said minimally, preferring not to give him a mental picture of her nudity. "It'll be at least fifteen minutes."

A pause, then, "Would you mind if I came in and got my electric shaver?"

"I would mind very much. I'm not—decent."

A moment passed before he responded, then, "Could you get decent? It'll just take a second."

Her impatience rose. "We're going to have to work out a schedule so this doesn't keep happening," she shouted.

"Good idea," he said. "So, is that a yes or a no?"

"A yes or a no about what?"

"About coming in?"

This guy's pushiness was enough to give any sane person the screaming meemies. She wanted to tell him exactly where he could go, with her blessing, but decided not to fight it. He'd only keep knocking and harping on about his dratted shaving kit until he got his way. Heaving a groan, she called, "Just a second." She unlocked the door that led to his bedroom, then stepped into the tub and drew the plastic curtain around her. "Okay, come in and get it over!"

"Thanks." His door opened. "I appreciate it."

"Whatever! Just hurry." As she wrapped herself more securely in her green, plastic cocoon, she looked at him and her eyes went wide. "You're not decent!"

He was about to retrieve his shaving gear from a drawer under the sink when she spoke. He stilled and glanced in her direction. "The hell I'm not." He straightened and spread his arms, displaying his bare upper torso, which, she was sorry to notice, showed off fantastic pectorals and a shamelessly trim and sexy stomach. His hip area was covered, barely, by a towel that started too far below his navel and ended provocatively high on the thighs. Roth Jerric had a decidedly cruel streak.

"Okay, you're *minutely* decent," she said grimly.

His forehead crinkled as though he'd been slapped. "For the record, Miss Hudson, men have a particular aversion to being alluded to as minute."

"Your glaring male insecurities are not my problem, Mr. Jerric." She freed an arm to indicate his "minute" attire. "What is that thing, a hankie?"

"Funny." He gave the shower curtain she'd wrapped herself up in a slow perusal. "Now I have a question for you." When he returned his attention to her face he watched her with eyes that missed nothing and revealed less. "You're wrapped in plastic."

"That's not a question."

"Okay. Let's try this." He indicated her with flick of his hand. "That's your idea of getting decent?"

"At least *I'm* covered."

"Yes." He nodded. "You are." He crossed his arms with languid, muscled grace she wished she could dismiss without a foolish increase in her heart rate. "There's one flaw in your fashion statement, however."

"Really?" She clutched the curtain more tightly around her, hating being put on the defensive, especially by a man who thought of her as inferior. "What might that be?"

"I can see through the blasted thing," he said. "Am I making myself as clear as you are?"

Her poor overstimulated brain took an extra tick to grasp the truth. He could see *through* the plastic? "Oh—my—*Lord!*" She staggered away from the curtain, spun around and hugged the cold wall tile. "Get out!"

"One second." She heard a drawer open and close. "Give me a knock when you're through."

"*Get out!*" she shrieked. She would never be able to look the man in the face again. Though it had to have been only a couple of seconds, it seemed like forever before his door closed with a solid thud. Quivery and shamed, she sank down and huddled in the depths of the cold iron tub. Drawing up her knees, she hugged them. How could she have been such a dimwit, wrapping herself in plastic like a piece of beef? Didn't she know better?

Or was there something cunningly sinister about Roth Jerric that caused female brains to short out when he came into a room? Whichever it was, it didn't alter the fact that she was embarrassed to the marrow of her bones. This fiasco was almost on a par with being labeled mediocre. After a moment's reflection she shook her head. "No, this is worse, Hannah," she muttered. "Now he thinks you're an idiot."

Hannah's vow of avoiding Roth at all costs was struck another blow at breakfast, when she discovered she would be sitting elbow to elbow with the man. At least she wouldn't have to look at him. She could eat, keep her mouth shut and let Joan Peterson, Roth and the inn's one other guest keep the conversation flowing. Her plan was to remain mute, eat as quickly as possible and promptly escape.

She took her assigned seat and focused across the table at the dour-faced, female artist-type. She nodded a hello. The middle-aged woman eyed her without responding. Not a good sign. *Please let this stranger be a babbler,* she prayed, staring hopefully at the woman with long salt-and-pepper hair, pulled away from her thin face by a tie-dyed scarf. Or was it a paint rag? She wore a paint-spattered T-shirt and no bra. Though Hannah couldn't see her lower half, she guessed she had on jeans decorated with the same random splatters of paint. What did she do, throw her oils at canvases?

Hannah had a bad feeling that the artist wasn't much of a talker. On the upside, she knew Joan to be an avid conversationalist. They'd met online in a chat room. It had been a time when Hannah had felt terribly vulnerable, right after her resignation. She'd needed to pour out her heart, and an anonymous online chat room seemed like as good a place as any.

Their fortuitous meeting and acquaintanceship had blossomed into an online friendship, resulting in Hannah winning this free stay. In all honesty, she had doubts that this trip was an actual "win" in any real contest. She sensed it was more like a good deed. She'd gotten to know Joan well enough to know she was extremely kindhearted and caring.

Whatever the catalyst, the "prize" came in the mail in the form of a coupon to be redeemed "in person" at the Blue Moon Inn. At the time Hannah had been so unhappy, how could she refuse a free, two-week stay on Oklahoma's most beautiful lake? It was a dream come true.

She sighed wistfully. If only Roth Jerric had gone anyplace else in the world for his vacation, it would have been perfect. *He could afford anyplace in the world,* she grumbled mentally. She reached for the coffee carafe at the same instant Roth did. Their hands touched. She felt a shock and an odd disorientation. "Excuse me," she mumbled, withdrawing her hand.

"No problem." He lifted the coffee and poured her a cup. "Cream?" he asked, as he gave himself a cup and passed the carafe to Mrs. Peterson, who had just seated herself.

Hannah shook her head but couldn't seem to respond. He smelled good, like sandalwood and leather.

"Cream?" he asked again, his hand hovering over the small ironstone pitcher. Apparently he didn't notice her head shake. "No," she said, more forcefully than necessary.

Both the artist and Joan glanced her way, appearing concerned. She cleared her throat and smiled lamely. At least she could talk again. "No, thank you," she repeated levelly, without looking at Roth.

"I'll have some," Joan said. "I love lots of good, honest, real cream in my coffee. None of those nondairy, nonfat, non-taste counterfeits for me or my guests." After pouring herself a healthy shot, she placed the container between her plate and the artist's, then she broke off a piece of ham and leaned down, looking below the table. "Here, Missy Mis, now be a good girl and don't beg."

"I don't eat fat," the artist said, her voice low and husky as a man's.

Joan glanced toward the thin, austere woman. "Mona, dear, I'm aware of that. But you're a fine artist, so I forgive you that shortcoming." She patted Mona's knobby hand. "Have we all met each other?" She glanced at Hannah and Roth.

"Hannah and I have met," Roth said.

Joan's expression closed for the briefest second. "Yes, I recall." Her smile returned, though not as jolly. "This is Mona Natterly, a frequent visitor." She patted Mona's hand again. "Every year she abides with me for the entire summer, then an occasional stopover during the rest of the year." Joan indicated the couple across from the artist. "Mona, this is Hannah Hudson, my dear Internet friend and this…" She hesitated, giving Roth a peculiarly disapproving look. Or did she? It was so brief Hannah couldn't be sure. "This is Ross—Johnson."

"Roth Jeric," he amended, smiling in Mona's direction. "Happy to meet you."

Just how do you know he's smiling, Hannah? She berated herself. *You promised yourself not to look at the man, and here you are staring at his profile.* She shifted her attention away.

"By the way, Ross," Joan went on, undeterred, "did you give my message to the sheriff?"

"He called."

The older woman looked perturbed. "He called? He didn't come out?"

"He had to respond to a wreck."

Joan sniffed. "Well, it's his loss."

"He said something odd on the phone—apologizing about the blue moon?"

Joan's attention had shifted to her coffee mug, but at the mention of the blue moon, she refocused on him. "As I said, it's his loss."

"What did he mean?" Roth prodded.

Hannah glanced his way, curious about the turn of the conversation. She scanned the side of his face, his sharp cheekbones, slightly arched nose and handsomely sculpted chin. Her gaze caught and held on the slashing dimple in his cheek, sinisterly charming.

"If you don't mind, I'd rather not discuss it now," Joan said, stiffly. "Perhaps in a few days, when I'm less crestfallen."

The remark surprised Hannah. She glanced at Joan. The elderly woman met her gaze then shifted her attention to Roth. "Fate has spoken." She sighed loudly. "I'll buck up." She patted Roth's hand. "I'm sure you're a nice man, Mr. Johnson."

"It's Jerric, but thanks," Roth said.

Hannah couldn't tell from his dry tone if Joan's eccentricity of continually botching his name annoyed him or if he was merely unsatisfied with her response. Nevertheless, she refused to check his expression. She'd stared at him more than enough for one morning. Disturbed that she'd noticed him at all, she forced herself to concentrate on her hostess. "Why are you crestfallen, Joan?"

The woman's smile grew melancholy. "Sweet girl, one of these days we'll sit down and have a good talk about—everything. But right now, forgive me. It's too close to my heart at the moment." She peered at Roth, then resumed eye contact with Hannah. "I just hope Madam Fate knows what she's doing," she said, regaining her pleasant expression. "Now, enjoy your breakfast. A sour disposition brings on a sour stomach, and I certainly don't want any sour stomachs at my inn."

"But—"

"Eat, dear," Joan cut in, then shifted her attention to the artist. "Mona, how is your oatmeal?"

"Fine."

Hannah lost hope that Mona would hold up her end of any conversation. She scanned the aging hippie's face, unable to decide how old she was. Her skin was leathery, as though she'd spent years outdoors. She might be thirty-five or fifty-five. "Do you paint landscapes?" she asked, assuming anybody as sun-dried as Mona must specialize in nature scenes.

Mona shifted her eyes from her oatmeal to Hannah. "I paint thoughts, musings, inklings," she said in that gravelly basso voice. She closed her eyes, as though listening to a lovely strain of music. "On those providential days when my muse is in ascension, I paint raw, unadulterated adoration."

"Yes," Joan said. "Yes, she does. Most exquisitely."

That was as clear as mud. "Oh…" Hannah wanted to ask more, like what in the world an "inkling" looked like, or what it took to get a muse into ascension, but she recalled her vow to be mute. So far, she hadn't done very well. She took up her fork. Apparently Mona got a special nonfat breakfast, since the rest of their plates were heaped with pancakes drenched in butter and syrup, a slab of ham on the side. Oh, well. She could diet when she got home. It wouldn't be hard, considering she was nearly broke. "Breakfast looks good," she said, then remembered her vow of muteness. *Don't be so hard on yourself,* she told herself inwardly. *A compliment to the cook is no great crime.*

"Why, thank you, dear."

Hannah took a bite, deciding if she had food in her mouth she would be less likely to babble. Why did Roth Jerric have to smell so nice? And why did his elbow have to brush her arm? Every time it did, she experienced a troubling flutter in her chest.

"I serve pancakes a lot. They're a special favorite of most guests. As are my egg dishes. Especially my spicy *Eggs à la Peterson, sunny-side up.*" When she said "up" she threw her hands over her head for emphasis. The move startled Hannah, already so nervous she jumped. Why did it have to be just as she lifted her coffee mug? The resulting lurch sloshed coffee on Roth's pancakes.

"Oh…shoot!" That's all she needed, to have to face the guy and apologize for ruining his breakfast. She did it as quickly and with as little eye contact as possible. "Sorry." She plunked her mug down and hefted her plate toward him. "Have mine. I'm not hungry."

"No need," he said.

"I insist." She scooted her chair back so abruptly it nearly overturned. Roth caught it just in time. She could feel his gaze, but she kept her focus on Joan. "I'm not feeling well."

"Goodness." Joan pushed awkwardly up to stand. "You're sick?"

"No." Hannah circled to the back of her chair. "Just—just…" She held up a halting hand. "Sit down, Joan. I—it's a headache. I'll take an aspirin and lie down for a bit. I'll be fine."

"Are you sure?" The proprietress looked worried. "I hope I didn't bring it on with all my complaining."

Joan reminded Hannah of her favorite grandmother, so willing to sacrifice for others. She managed a smile of encouragement. "You're not responsible at all. Besides, I can't recall you doing any complaining. Please, eat your breakfast."

"Well…" Joan lowered herself to her chair, clearly reluctant.

Hannah belatedly noticed Roth had stood up. What was he doing? She glanced at him, at his face, his eyes, breaking her vow to smithereens. He not only smelled intoxicating but he looked it, in that torso-hugging, sky-blue knit shirt and those formfitting jeans. She'd never seen him in jeans before, not even on casual Fridays. He looked scrumptious—and very serious. She wondered what went on behind that frown. Did he doubt her headache story? "Sit down," she said, upset with herself for her smashed vow, and worse, thinking of him as scrumptious. "Eat my pancakes."

He said nothing, merely watched her. She was positive he

felt her alleged headache was open to question. So what if he was right? It was none of his business if she wanted to lie about having a headache. *It's a free country, Mr. Jerric,* she threw out silently. *Believe me or don't believe me. I couldn't care less.* "Excuse me, everybody." She dashed out of the dining room, into the foyer and up the stairs.

An hour later, Hannah considered leaving her room. Maybe it was safe. Surely by now breakfast was over and Roth was busy doing whatever he came to the inn to do—fishing, boating, making other people feel inferior. She pushed off the bed and walked to her balcony door, overlooking a quiet cove some one hundred feet down a gentle, tree-lined slope. She couldn't hear the lapping of the water from this distance, but somewhere out on the lake she heard the drone of an approaching motorboat.

Through branches she thought she could see a sailboat. Yes, there it was, its white sail billowing in the wind. She opened the multipaned door, feeling a little better, and took a deep breath of fresh air. The day would be warm. June had been unseasonably cool, but July in Oklahoma could see temperatures soaring to three digits. Soon the weather would be too hot for open windows and enjoying fresh breezes off the lake.

A knock at her door exploded her positive mood. She recognized the force of that knock. It had to be Roth Jerric. Closing her eyes, she took in another breath of fresh, country air. "What now?"

"How are you feeling?"

She wanted to tell him the truth, that she felt depressed, and a great deal of her depression had to do with him. "If you mean the headache, I'm fine."

"Can I come in?"

She didn't want a one-on-one with him, especially not in her bedroom, so she decided to lie. "I'm not decent." She winced, the off-the-cuff statement echoing the bathroom disaster. Couldn't she come up with something else? Like the truth, *I've been crying, a direct result of how insecure your low opinion of me has made me.*

She'd had great respect and admiration for Roth when she worked at Jerric Oil. Knowing he, in particular, thought her mediocre had become a huge roadblock to her self-confidence. Running head-on into the man at the Blue Moon Inn had been far from therapeutic.

"Could we possibly do this on the same side of the door?" he shouted.

"What do you want?"

"To speak to you."

"Must you?"

A full half minute of silence ticked by, then, "I'll only take a second. Please, open the door."

She felt foolish and a little childish. Did strong, independent women cower behind locked doors? Not on your life! She straightened her shoulders. She was no coward. It was one thing to be upset, but quite another to wallow in self-pity. "Oh—just a second."

She hurried to the old oak dresser, grabbed a tissue, dabbed at her eyes and blew her nose. Stuffing the tissue in her jeans pocket, she pulled her face powder from the top drawer and patted the puff across her nose and cheeks. "I'm slipping something on." She closed the drawer and gave herself a once-over in the mirror. Her red nose camouflaged by face powder, she looked composed. She ran her fingers through her curls, fluffing them. Roth was only an ex-boss, just a man. Why get all caught up in *his* opinion? "Coming."

She opened the door, determined to remain formal and solemn. Neither he nor his estimation of her were important. Unfortunately, seeing him sent a rush of ambivalence through her. He was quite a sight standing there all tall, intensely serious and excruciatingly handsome. His features carried a startling lack of information. A slight sideways movement of his jaw indicated impatience, perhaps. Or possibly some internal burden he carried that had nothing to do with her. Cheek muscles stood out, telegraphing the fact that he clenched his jaw. "Thanks," he said, at last.

She shored up her indignation with the lift of her chin. "What is it?"

"Joan has your breakfast warming in the oven."

"I told you to eat my breakfast since I ruined yours."

"I ate my own. The coffee didn't hurt it."

She refused to feel guilty. He was a big boy. He made his own decisions. "Whatever." She turned away and walked to her open balcony door. Up close he smelled too good. She needed the fortification of neutral country air. "Thanks for the bulletin," she said lightly. "My curiosity was killing me."

For a moment he didn't say anything. She hoped he was gone, but had a nagging suspicion he wasn't. "I thought we might work on that schedule," he said.

She clenched her teeth on a curse. Schedule? What was he…suddenly it came back to her. Not only must she face him again, but they had to discuss the bathroom schedule, which would be a terrific way to relive the plastic fiasco. For her own sanity, she continued to stare at the placid lake. "Let's say—" she thought fast "—from the top of the hour to the half hour the bathroom is yours. From the half hour to the top of the next hour, it's mine. I stay out the first half of every hour and you stay out the second half. That way, any time of the day or night, we know when the bathroom is ours and we can avoid each other at our leisure. How's that?" She had to admit, it wasn't a bad suggestion, considering it was off the top of her head. She clamped her hands together, waiting.

"Sounds good," he said.

She swallowed, more relieved than she wanted to admit. A surge of satisfaction dashed through her at the small but satisfying success. "Fine. Now, go away."

After a beat, he said, "Look, Miss Hudson, I don't know what problem you have with me, but if you don't mind a little frankness, I'm no more interested in being around you than you are in being around me."

He grew quiet, and she wondered if that was her cue to speak. She stared at nothing, all her senses focused on the man standing behind her on her threshold. "Great," she said. "I'm thrilled neither of us wants anything to do with the other."

"Now that that's out in the open," he said, "have a nice stay."

"Have a nice life," she shot back, then lowered her voice to a whisper. *"Arrogant ass."*

Roth turned away from Hannah's door, muttering, "Prickly witch."

He went down the stairs into the front lobby. At a loose end, he didn't know what to do. Restless, he strode into the dining room and grabbed a mug off the sideboard where a coffee urn sat. He filled his cup with the strong, steaming brew and stood there thinking. How did he go about doing what he'd come here to do?

As a youth, he'd wanted to be a builder, a creator. His oil company came about as a fluke, his natural abilities setting him on a course so successful he lost sight of earlier, creative aspirations. His inner struggle ate at him, his disillusion with the conflict between his youthful dreams and what became the reality of his life.

Last night's meeting in the garden with Hannah only made matters worse, with her reference to arm candy. Roth knew full well what arm candy was. Even closed down emotionally, in his bloodless way, since his divorce he'd enjoyed plenty of it. And before that, his wife, Janice, had been a striking woman, but never, ever in his mind "arm candy."

He'd been the envy of any man who saw her on his arm, and he'd felt like the luckiest guy in the world. He'd loved her absolutely, blindly, as it turned out. After the tragedy of their infant son's crib death, Roth suggested they try again for another child, but Janice refused. Roth could still feel the blow of her rejection, even all these years later.

The birth of their child, Colin, made her realize she didn't like being pregnant, didn't want her body "distorted" again. The worst shock of all was when she said the death of their baby was a blessing in disguise.

A blessing in disguise?

Every time he thought about her twisted intellectualizing that any child's death could be a blessing, he felt sick. Suddenly unsteady, he grasped the sideboard for support. Janice was so nonchalant, so cold and analytical, while he grieved intensely. Her decision left him feeling not only grief of loss, but betrayed.

That was when he finally saw her for what she was, all appearance and no substance. At that moment he knew their marriage was over. He was the only one mourning, the only one who wanted a traditional home, with children. Disillusioned and embittered by Janice's rejection and the fallibility of his own insights where personal relationships were concerned, he shut himself down, became obsessed with work, determined to feel nothing. Women to him became diversions, nothing more.

He heard sounds, rousing him from his morbid mental detour. He lifted his head, alert. What was that?

"Mona, don't fret," a voice said. "I won't start requiring you to pay for your stays. Don't be absurd."

That was obviously Joan's voice, growing nearer.

"But this letter," Mona said.

"Oh, dear, where did you get that?"

"I needed a scrap to make a list of paints I want to order, and I found it in the trash."

"That's where it belongs."

"But, it says you're broke and you could lose the inn." Mona sounded worried.

"My banker is an old worrywart." Joan paused. "Besides, Mr. Johnson is a paying guest."

Roth lifted his mug in a mock salute. "It's Jerric, Roth Jerric," he wisecracked, under his breath. "But feel free to call me Ross."

"What about the other one? The girl?"

"Hannah? Oh, I sent her one of my coupons for a free, two-week stay." After a second, she added bleakly, "I had such plans for her. She's a lovely women and she has no job. I certainly wouldn't ask her to pay. Just as I would never ask you."

"But if the bank takes your inn—"

"Pish tosh! Think no more about it."

He heard a dog yap.

"Hush, Missy Mis. Now, see what you made me do? Missy Mis hates it when I raise my voice. Let's speak of more pleasant things."

"Changing the subject won't erase the problem, Joan."

"It's not a problem, Mona, merely a banker's preoccupation with minutia."

"This letter is not minutia. It's serious. Perhaps you could sell some of the paintings I've given you over the years."

"Mona, I love your work. They're marvelous. *Genius.* But sadly, guests and locals fail to understand your gift as I do. Now don't get moody. You know your muse can't ascend when you're moody." Her sigh was audible. They were right around the corner. Roth didn't want to embarrass his hostess by having her discover he had overheard about her financial trouble.

Quietly he carried his mug through the lobby into the parlor. His footfalls were muted by the Oriental rug as he crossed the room to take a seat on a fusty, rose-colored sofa. He focused on the placid lake outside the picture window, aware when the women came into the foyer. Without noticing him, they continued their hushed conversation down the center hallway toward the rear of the house.

He sat back, contemplating Joan's money troubles. He felt

a pang of sympathy for her. It must be terrible to be elderly and financially insecure. He'd seen and heard enough to know that Joan was a kindhearted philanthropist, but without the financial wherewithal to be so openhanded.

If her income rested solely on the meager amount she asked of her guests, she was no businesswoman. The place was far from palatial, but he wouldn't have been surprised if she'd quoted him double what she did, even for such drab accommodations. The lake access and view, alone, were worth twice what she charged.

He thought about this morning and his brush with Hannah Hudson's nudity and found himself almost smiling. *Bad boy,* he told himself. You must not enjoy that memory—it was a terrible moment for her. Yet, it certainly made the accommodations—sharing a bathroom—far less aggravating. If he were to be totally honest, it made sharing her bathroom worth every half hour he would be barred from its entry.

He experienced an uncomfortable upsurge of lust and shifted in his seat. How had his thoughts skipped so radically from impoverished Joan Peterson to lovely, if explosive, Hannah Hudson? Enough of that. Besides, he had not come here for the sport of conquest, which was moot anyway, since Miss Hudson exhibited as much delight in discovering he was there as she might show a poisonous snake found coiled in her bed.

He forced his mind to the less inflammatory subject—Joan Peterson's money troubles. He supposed it was none of his business, but the conversation between the two women nagged.

He thought of Joan as a nice, if eccentric woman, and though he tried to numb his emotions, especially soft ones like pity, empathy or love, he felt sorry for her. He even experienced an urge to help. He sensed she would be too proud to accept charity. She couldn't even accept that she had financial trouble. So, how might he be of assistance?

He stood, lifted his mug from the doilied end table, ambled

aimlessly into the lobby and out the front door onto the wide porch. After a few minutes, he found himself on the lakeside of the inn, strolling along a gravel path through towering walnut, oak and pecan trees on his way toward the shoreline. He recalled so well, as a child, times he had dashed, barefoot, to the water's edge. On the run, he'd thrown himself into a racing dive, skimming the shallows to gain deeper water beyond the cove. Today Grand Lake teamed with speedboats, large and small, plus sailboats and little wave-runners, buzzing all over the lake like water-bound motorcycles. The cove wasn't buoyed to warn boaters away. Swimmers venturing too far out onto the lake these days would be foolhardy.

Yet, with the buffering cove, a sense of privacy and sanctuary endured, just as it had in his boyhood. Around the bend, Roth knew where the water deepened enough for docks. His family never owned a motorboat, just a rowboat. So they had no use for a fancy dock. Wondering if anyone had put in a dock, he veered off the lawn into the woods, deciding to see for himself. He had a feeling no one had, or there would be a clearing through the heavy underbrush.

When he reached the spot and came out of the trees, he picked his way down a rocky slope toward the lake. The sunshine felt good; the air smelled fresh with the cool breeze coming off the water. He experienced a spark of exhilaration, something he hadn't felt in a long time.

"What if…" He reached a rocky ledge and leaned against a huge old oak. He remembered this tree, and this ledge. As a youth he had dived into the deep water a thousand times from this very spot. He smiled at the recollection. After a time of quiet contemplation, his mind began to teem with hints, sketches of the potential for what might be a promising adventure. An adventure that would not only benefit him, but would put Joan Peterson's financial troubles to rest for good and all.

His enthusiasm grew as his vision became more and more

solid in his mind. This was exactly what he needed, the creative redemption of his soul. The very reason he came back to his childhood home.

He caught sight of a crane, its snowy wings spread wide as it circled above the calm, blue water. With a laugh, he shouted out, "Who says you can't go home again?"

CHAPTER THREE

ROTH returned to the inn well into his mental blueprints. He knew this idea was right for him, because of the way it fell so readily into place. He would buy the inn and develop the lake property into a resort with a marina, dock rentals and a gated, lakeside community that included a high-rise condo. The lower floors with less grand views would provide midrange housing for families unable to afford the offered lakeshore lots. Upper floor plans would provide high-dollar dwellings for affluent couples not wanting the hassle of a yard, opting to pay a premium for lofty lake vistas.

Joan Peterson would never again have to worry about money. Though her home would have to be razed, he would provide her with a sleek, new condominium as part of the deal.

He found his hostess in the kitchen, tying on an apron, about to begin the preparations for their midday meal. He checked his watch. Only ten o'clock and already she had to begin the drudgery of meal preparation. Poor woman. How fortunate for her that his plan would put an end to the ceaseless grind of running the aging inn. She was getting too old to maintain the sort of pace it took to keep the place clean and put food on the table. He felt extremely benevolent about his plan. He hadn't felt so at one with the universe in years. Joan Peterson had a wonderful surprise coming.

Thirty minutes later, Roth's harmonious mood had darkened considerably.

"No, no, no, *no!*" Joan cried, though Roth had just explained, for the third time, how much his plans for her property benefited her. Miss Mischief, curled on an oval rag-rug in a corner, sat up and began to yap. Joan made a quelling motion toward the mutt, and it magically ceased its racket. "I will never sell my inn," she said less piercingly, more to keep her dog quiet than a decline in her agitation. "It's my home. How many times must I tell you, Mr. Johnson, I would *never* feel comfortable living in some highfalutin condominium." She turned away and began to chop an onion, her gnarled hands amazingly adroit as she severed it on a wooden board so worn by years its center was a rough-hewn valley.

Roth was accustomed to Joan referring to him as Ross Johnson, and let it go. The important thing was to make her face facts. "Don't you understand? If you lose the inn to the bank, it will go on the market. I could buy it then, at a bargain price. Why shouldn't you benefit—"

"Don't be ridiculous!" Her knife whacked the onion to bits. "The bank isn't going to take my inn. Where did you get such an idea?"

He hadn't eavesdropped on purpose, but he felt guilty anyway. He shook it off. "I overheard your conversation with Mona."

Joan continued to chop the onion for another few seconds without comment. Finally she lay the knife aside and peered at him, her eyes magnified behind her spectacles. He saw pain glittering there. "I'm ashamed of you."

He felt like he was being reprimanded by his own grandmother, long dead, but a kinder person he'd never known. He experienced another stab of guilt at his misconduct. "I apologize, but if you look at it another way, the incident was providential. Don't you understand? I can help. By purchasing your property, I can take away your financial troubles forever."

She blinked then shook her head. He watched moisture gather in her eyes and he feared she was near tears. "What you want to do is take away my home."

"Only this old house. You'll have a home. A wonderful, modern home without peeling paint and rusty pipes."

She sniffed. Her lips lifted at the corners, the expression pitying. "*This* is my home, and it will be until I die. I'm sorry you find it so—so unpalatable."

"That's not what I meant to imply—"

She held up a halting hand. "No, hear me out," she cut in. "I want you to understand."

He didn't like the turn of this conversation, but he nodded, knowing he had no choice. The best arguments could only be made when you knew the opposition inside out. "All right," he said, but silently added, *It doesn't matter how poignant your life story is, the facts remain the same. Your inn is about to be taken away from you, no matter what you want or how many tears you shed.*

"You see, I met my husband here." She indicated the direction of the church ruins. "In that garden. I was twenty-one and quite the independent lass." Her expression softened as she recalled the story . "I had been hiking and got so caught up in the beauty of the countryside, I got lost. It was long after dark by then, but a lovely, warm June night. Fifty years ago, northeastern Oklahoma wasn't nearly as built-up as it is now. The Grand River dam was so new, I could have wandered for days without finding a human being."

A faraway look came into her eyes; a genuine smile curved her lips as she relived a happier time. "Around midnight, I chanced on this private home where we now stand. Being very late, I didn't want to disturb the family, so I rested on a stone bench among the church ruins. When I looked up to scan the heavens, to my amazement a full moon sat squarely in the center of an arched opening in the church wall. I was so transfixed,

I didn't hear a man approach. When he stood directly behind me, he spoke. I shall never forget what he said.

"'That happens once in a blue moon,' he said. His voice was soft and low, almost like an angel's, if an angel spoke as a human man. I was startled but strangely unfearful. I turned toward him. There and then, I saw the face of my soul mate, Durham Peterson." She grew still, swallowed several times, as though the memory stirred deep, poignant emotions.

"We were married within weeks," she went on. "Soon afterward, Dur confessed a desire to travel the world. An adventurer myself, I gladly agreed. Dur had a comfortable inheritance, so for the next forty years we lived a charmed life. Then nine years ago, after Dur was taken from me in a tragic fall while we were mountain climbing in Nepal, I found my way back to the stone bench in that same garden. Being there comforted me. The property had changed hands a number of times in all those years and was abandoned, boarded up. With what remained of our money, I bought it.

"Repairing the house took more capital than I counted on, so in order to make ends meet, I decided to take in boarders, because..." She hesitated and looked away. After a moment, she once again trained her attention on him, her expression determined. "...because, Mr. Johnson, I knew I had come home for good. And since I met my beloved Durham on that magical night of a blue moon, I named my home the Blue Moon Inn." She scanned her kitchen and ran a loving hand over the scratched, green-tiled countertop. "I would rather die than sell." She shook her head, adamant. "I won't allow those magical ruins to be torn down. Not *ever.*"

"Magical ruins," he muttered.

"Yes, magical," she repeated, steel behind her words. "I believe the enchantment of the full moon was the sire of my bliss with Durham, and I feel sure any couple caught in the light of that miraculous phenomenon will be likewise blessed."

He frowned, the blue moon riddle falling together. Apparently the romantically kooky Mrs. Peterson had intended that the sheriff and Hannah Hudson be caught in the blue moon's light, and because of some lunar power she conjured in her head, they would *poof* become a loving couple. Evidently, in her mind, when the sheriff was detained, the blue moon moved out of its witchy window of opportunity. That had to be the reason for her crestfallen remark at breakfast.

He'd never heard such romantic drivel in his life. Obviously the woman lived in her own wacky dream world, where neither the consequences of missing mortgage payments nor basic common sense dared to tread.

"Tearing down my home and those hallowed ruins would be sacrilege, Mr. Johnson. Pure sacrilege." She scooped up the chopped onion and sidled to the nearby stove where oil sizzled in a pot. She dumped in the onions and the sizzling intensified. Steam poured from the pot. "Please excuse me, but I'm *enormously* busy. You wouldn't want dinner to be late. I serve it precisely at noon." She gave him a pleasant smile that didn't pretend to reach her eyes, then motioned him off with a shooing gesture. "Go. Enjoy the day," she said, once again presenting her cheery hostess manners. To her, the subject of the sale of her inn was closed.

"Smile, dear boy." She patted his jaw; the strong scent of raw onions assailed his nostrils. "I never allow guests at my inn to get dyspepsia from stress or worry. Go, relax. There's a lovely porch swing out front. Or as you're a young, strong buck, perhaps you'd rather take a brisk swim. Work off some of that excess energy. There's plenty of time before dinner."

He stared at her, nonplussed that anybody could be so blind to such an obvious godsend as his offer. Anyone with a molecule of sense would grab his deal, sob for joy and most likely kiss his shoes while doing it. But this woman acted as though he were trying to buy her firstborn child. Idiotic!

Joan shuffled away from him disappearing into the kitchen pantry. She began to hum, as though her money problems could be dispensed with as adroitly as she carved up that onion. Shaking his head, he walked out of the kitchen. If Joan Peterson thought the discussion was over, she was daffier than he gave her credit for.

Dinner and supper were difficult for Hannah, being near Roth. Though she kept her attention diverted from his face, she could feel the tension crackling between them. As a matter of fact, she felt so much tension it seemed to extend beyond the two of them. But that was crazy. She had no bone to pick with either Joan or Mona. And she had the distinct impression that the two women were longtime friends. The idea that animosity smoldered between them seemed remote. At both meals the two talked enough to prove their affinity was real.

As for tension between Roth and either of the women, well, it seemed implausible. Mona spent much of her time out behind the remaining church wall, flinging paint at artist canvases. That afternoon Hannah found out the hard way when she reck lessly rounded the old stone wall without checking for airborne oils, and got slimed with vermilion.

The experience had been no great tragedy. After the initial shock, she managed to laugh, amazing, considering her circumstances. The shorts and tank top she wore were so faded and tired she decided a flourish of crimson gave them the perfect touch of character.

Her hair was a different story. Luckily the bathroom schedule she and Roth had worked out favored her at that moment. After Mona doused her head and exposed skin with linseed oil, she still held legitimate bathroom rights for twenty minutes. Plenty of time to soak in the tub and rid herself of flammable linseed fumes.

Besides dinner and supper, Hannah had managed to avoid

Roth. Even so, she couldn't sleep. Simply knowing he was a room away gave her insomnia. After tossing and turning until midnight, she gave up trying to sleep and decided to raid the refrigerator. Sitting beside the man at the dining table had cut into her appetite. She had barely picked at her food. Slipping into terry scuffs and throwing on her knee-length cotton robe, she tiptoed toward the staircase.

Halfway down the steps she heard a female voice coming from the parlor and recognized it as Joan Peterson. But to whom was she speaking? Hannah couldn't make out what she said, since she spoke in low murmurings. She eased on down the stairs, her curiosity aroused. When she reached the foyer, she crept to the parlor door, experiencing a surge of guilt. She wasn't ordinarily a nosy person, but she sensed someone was upset and felt she would be remiss if she could help and didn't. At the door she was surprised to see Joan sitting alone on the sofa. She'd been speaking, but to whom? Her dog lay curled beside her, its scruffy head in her lap. Apparently she was talking to the animal.

"Such a bothersome man." She stroked Miss Mischief's back. "How dare he threaten to steal my home out from under me!"

"Who's threatening to steal your home?" The question burst out of Hannah before she could stop it.

Joan jerked around. Miss Mischief's head popped up and she yapped. The older woman's hands flew to her breast. "Gracious," she cried. "You frightened the life out of me."

Hannah felt awful and rushed into the parlor. "I'm so sorry, Mrs. Peterson." She rounded the sofa to perch beside the dog. Leaning across the aging pet, she touched Joan's knee fondly. "I heard a voice and out of curiosity I checked it out. I just wanted to make sure everything was okay. Then, just as I got within earshot, you spoke of somebody threatening you. I reacted—hastily, I'm afraid." She experienced a burning flush in her cheeks. "It's a character flaw—reacting on reflex."

How many times had she wished she could keep a cooler head? Sadly, after so many years of flinging herself onto live emotional grenades—for what, at that instant, seemed right and necessary—she held out little hope of repairing that particular flaw. She released Joan's knee and clenched her hands in her lap. "Forgive my meddling, but I truly would like to help, if I can."

Recovering from her shock, Joan smiled and placed her work-roughened hand over Hannah's fingers. "I have a flaw, too. Talking to myself—or little Missy Mis, here." She hesitated, then glanced away. "Or to Dur, my beloved. He was so sensible. He could see things clearly. Without him, I—I sometimes feel very lost…" Her words trailed away.

Hannah's heart went out to the woman. She felt herself near tears, which stunned her. Was this emotional assault a sentimental reaction to the glimpse of the depth of Joan's love for a man with whom she shared most of her life? Or was it simply a build-up of stress combined with lack of sleep?

Joan's profile blurred. Hannah blinked to clear her vision. Someone was trying to steal Joan's home. She needed to pull herself together. She had a decent, logical mind. Why not take a stab at putting it to better use than wallowing in her troubles? "Please, tell me who's threatened you."

Hannah's request drew Joan back from wherever she had gone in her head. She faced the younger woman. "Oh, it wasn't quite as nasty as that," Joan said, though her expression held no love for the idea. "He made a smooth, businesslike offer to buy my home, my property, and when I refused, he wouldn't let it go. He pushed and pushed. Finally he as much as said if I didn't sell he could get it for practically nothing once the bank foreclosed." She withdrew a handkerchief from her apron pocket and swiped at her nose. "Adding insult to injury, he said my pipes are noisy and—and, well I'd rather not think about it."

"Who?" Hannah asked, now angry on Mrs. Peterson's behalf. "Who said such a horrible thing to you? Your inn is—is just *fine.*" That wasn't quite true. The inn needed work, but that wasn't what Joan longed to hear right now.

"Why, that Mr. Johnson, of course."

"Johnson?"

"Yes. The man in the room next to you."

Roth Jerric! Now it made sense. Her anger intensified. The man was indefensible, intimidating an old woman! She squeezed Joan's shoulders with real affection. "That man thinks everything and everyone is below par, except him." She tried to look encouraging though resentment, restlessness and fatigue were taking a toll. The man was a walking plague, a spirit-crushing virus. "His opinion of your inn isn't worth stewing over."

"You think so?" Joan dabbed at her eyes with her hankie. "I must admit, lately I've had to let some repairs slide, but I try to keep a clean, happy inn."

"And you do," Hannah said. When Joan took a deep breath and smiled tremulously, she felt her encouraging words had helped. But she had to know what was behind this, if there was any truth to the foreclosure revelation. "Is the inn in financial trouble?" It wouldn't surprise her. Exterior paint was peeling. The wood floors badly needed refinishing. Plumbing squeaked and groaned whenever water was run anyplace in the house. Furnishings, rugs and fixtures showed wear that would be off-putting to many vacationers.

"There isn't a shred of truth to the idea that I'm in financial straits." Joan went back to stroking her dog's back. "Not really. My banker is a worrywart, that's all." She shrugged hunched shoulders. "That Mr. Johnson spied on a private conversation between Mona and me. He overheard us speaking about a letter from the bank. Later he confronted me, pressing me unmercifully," she said. "I know you and he are smitten, but—"

"Smitten?" Hannah echoed, stunned. "Hardly! I think he's a

pompous, self-satisfied SOB who thinks way too highly of his own opinions," she said, her tone hard. "Don't let him bully you."

Now it was Joan's turn to look stunned. "You—you mean you and he aren't intoxicated with each other?"

"Definitely not! I'd have to be cockeyed drunk to spend five minutes alone with him just *talking*." Hannah made a disgusted sound in her throat. "He's practically the last person on earth I wanted to see here."

"You mean you knew him before?"

"Unfortunately I did," she said. "He was my boss at Jerric Oil. To be frank, the sight of him revolts me." That was a lie. The sight of him didn't revolt her a bit. Ironically the sight of him made her heart skip. It wasn't the sight of him that was the problem—or maybe it was. For a logical, rational person, she wasn't at her most logical and rational lately. Too much of her mental turmoil she could lay directly at his feet. His negative appraisal of her had ripped a huge hole in her self-esteem.

"I don't see how that can be," Joan said.

Confused, Hannah gave Joan her full attention. "What?"

"I don't see how you two aren't falling madly in love."

Hannah listened with troubled diligence, struggling to make sense of Joan's remark. "Why on earth…" She shook her head, baffled. "Why would you think such a thing?"

"Because you two were bathed in the magical light of the blue moon together. It's fate."

"Fate?" Hannah repeated, disconcerted by the conviction on the older woman's face.

Joan nodded. "My darling Dur and I met exactly that way— in the light of the blue moon. It shone through the old church window. We immediately fell in love and were happy together through all our married years."

Hannah took a big breath, relieved. It was nothing more than a romantic superstition brought on by Joan's imagination and the novel way she met her husband. With a compassionate smile, she said, "That's a lovely story. I'm thrilled that you and Dur were so happy." She withdrew her arm from around Joan's shoulders. "If you'll permit me to make a suggestion, I think your happiness was due more to your natural compatibility than lunar love rays beamed through a hole in an old wall."

Joan's forehead crinkled as though she didn't appreciate Hannah's flippancy about a phenomenon she held dear. She felt guilty for belittling Joan's blue moon fantasy and hurriedly added, "I'm only saying, because it was magical for you, doesn't necessarily mean it would be for every couple."

Joan seemed to consider that as she trained her attention on her dog and continued to stroke it. "I'm not convinced." She peered at Hannah. "Are you positive you have no warm feelings toward Mr. Johnson, and he has none for you?"

Hannah experienced a tingle of squeamishness. It wasn't as though she actually intended to lie. Just because Roth was handsome and her pulse jumped when he came into a room, didn't mean she had so-called "warm" feelings for him. At least not the kind of warm feelings that led to marriage. Maybe to a night of unthinking lust, but that was all. She shook herself to banish such wayward ideas. "I would rather cuddle up to a rattler." Since she knew for a documented fact that Roth Jerric held no great opinion of her, she added, "I sincerely doubt that I'm Mr. Jerric's type."

"How odd." Joan shook her head as though trying to grasp such an inconceivable concept. That wasn't surprising since she'd clung to the blue moon notion for much of her life. After a moment, Joan resumed eye contact with Hannah. "I'm not persuaded, you understand. But if there is even the slightest chance I'm wrong, perhaps all is not lost after all."

Hannah found herself confused again. "All what is not lost? I don't understand."

Joan smiled and seemed truly happy. "Nothing. Nothing at all. Just an old woman's ramblings." She lifted her pet up and set her on the rug. "Come along, Missy Mis. It's off to bed for us." She pushed awkwardly up from the sofa and faced Hannah. "I'm glad we had this chat." She absently smoothed her apron. "You've certainly pulled me out of the blues. I'll sleep, now."

I'm happy for you, Hannah threw out mentally. The conversation hadn't done much for her peace of mind. Falling in love with Roth Jerric? That was the stuff nightmares were made of.

Joan patted Hannah's shoulder. "You're a fine young woman. And though I cherish and believe in the blue moon magic, there is a little part of me that hopes you and Mr. Johnson aren't fated. You deserve…" She let the thought trail away and nodded. "Well, you do." With that bewildering statement she shuffled away, Miss Mischief pitter-pattering behind. "Good night, dear."

Hannah watched Joan walk out of the parlor and across the lighted foyer into the hallway leading to her quarters. After a few moments, she came out of her strange daze and shook her head. "I deserve— what?" she asked the empty room.

The silence was broken only by the mantel clock's rhythmic ticking. Hannah shifted in the direction of the hearth, empty and soot stained. Her stomach growled, reminding her why she had come downstairs. She stood up. "Right now I deserve a cold meat loaf sandwich," she told the clock. "And a tall, cold glass of milk."

As she headed to the kitchen, she thought about Joan's fantasy that she and Roth were fated to fall in love. "Yeah, right," she mumbled. "He's yearning for a love-match he can point to with pride and call mediocre. And I'm hot to hook up with an egotistical jerk who gets his jollies threatening to snatch sweet little old ladies' homes out from under them." She chuckled derisively. "Now, *that's* a blue moon match if I've ever heard one."

She came to a skidding halt in the kitchen doorway. She wasn't alone. The overhead light was off, leaving her no advanced warning that someone lurked in the kitchen's semi-darkness. A single, forty-watt bulb over the sink was lit, left on for the occasional late-night refrigerator raid. The dusky glow revealed an all-too-familiar presence. Not five feet away, Roth sat, facing her, on one of two benches drawn up to a battered table Joan used for meal preparation.

Evidently he'd been aware of her approach, for he lifted a glass of orange juice in a jesting salute. "Well, well, if it isn't the woman revolted by the sight of me."

She felt herself go foolishly light-headed by the way his deep, sexy voice affected her in the heavy silence, even as he mocked her. But worse, much worse, was the display of his broad, bare chest in the pale radiance. She prayed he wasn't bare below the waist, too.

After a second, she pulled herself together, hoping he didn't notice her momentary paralysis. Upset with herself for being affected at all, she took it out on him. "I guess I shouldn't be surprised you listened in on our private conversation. I understand it's your method of operation."

He replaced his glass on the table, resting his forearms and the flats of his hands on the tabletop. "It's not a big house, and you two weren't exactly whispering."

"You could have made yourself known," she said, deciding not to let his bothersome presence keep her from eating *again*. If she did she would end up dying of starvation. She headed toward the refrigerator, located at an angle that allowed her to reassure herself that he wore a pair of dark shorts.

To her dismay she could also see his legs. Though the tabletop placed them in deep shadow, she remembered vividly the time he wore that skimpy towel. His legs had not gone unnoticed. They were long and muscular. Even his ankles were sexy. She silently cursed him. "In case you don't know how to politely make yourself known," she said, trying to stay on track, "you say something like, 'Excuse me. I didn't mean to pry,' or at least clear your throat."

He surveyed her, his expression hard to read. If forced to guess his mood, she had to lean toward annoyed. "I hated to interrupt," he said, none too pleasantly. "You were being so colorful in your estimation of me." He broke eye contact and stared off, running a tapered finger over the juice glass. She experienced a shivery reaction at the sight of the small, skimming caress.

"Let's see, how did you put it?" he mused aloud, drawing her back. "I'm a pompous, self-satisfied SOB who thinks too highly of his own opinions?" He paused, as though concentrating, then nodded. "I believe that was it. And—oh, yes—you'd have to be cockeyed drunk to spend five minutes alone with me—just talking." He returned his attention to her face. A muscle jumped in his cheek. "I hope you're good and cockeyed, Miss Hudson. Otherwise…" He lifted his arm to make a show of looking at his watch. Tendons and muscles in his arm and shoulder played a fetching game with light and shadow. "Since I'm not planning to leave right away, you have three minutes of alone-time left."

She stared, galled by his baiting. How dare he throw her words back in a bid to tyrannize her. Well, it wasn't going to work. She struggled to keep her voice steady. "What I actually said was, you think *way* too highly of your own opinions. Way…too…highly," she repeated slowly, enunciating crisply to insure that he didn't underestimate her vast aversion to him.

She turned her back and yanked open the refrigerator. "I'll stay in this kitchen as long as I please. I said I'd have to be cockeyed drunk to spend five minutes alone with you *talking*. I don't have any intention of talking to you any further."

He didn't respond but she could feel his eyes ripping holes in her back. Shaky from the bite of his stare, she grabbed the pottery tray of leftover meat loaf and lifted it to the counter. She then dove back into the fridge for milk. From a cabinet beside the sink she plucked a tall glass and filled it.

The silence became a howling roar, painful to the point of being debilitating. She had trouble with her hands. They fumbled and shook. Annoyed that her absurd, physical reaction to the man could create so much silent havoc, she faced the fact that making a sandwich would require more agility than her jittery fingers could manage. Taking a knife from its butcher block holder, she whacked off a slab of meat and tossed it on a saucer.

Her back to Roth, she stood at the counter, pinched off pieces of the loaf, chewed and swallowed. Why couldn't she taste it? After a minute, she took a swallow of milk, which didn't have any taste, either. What was wrong? Could her body do nothing else, tend to no other chores—like taste bud duty—besides acknowledge the forbidding presence of Roth Jerric?

"That's too bad," he said.

She flinched at the unexpectedness of his remark but managed to get herself under control before a building scream escaped her throat. What in heaven's name did he mean by that? Against her will, she asked, "What's too bad?" Mad at herself for playing his game, she decided to put the remainder of the meat loaf back in the refrigerator. Her stomach wasn't feeling so good. To soothe the churning, she took another swig of milk.

"That you aren't speaking to me. It's too bad—since we're fated to fall in love."

Hannah choked and clunked her glass to the counter coughing. The spasm became so acute she found herself gasping. Hacking and panting, oxygen starved and dizzy, she planted her hands on the counter for support.

"Are you okay?"

Either her brain wasn't functioning well or his voice came from much nearer. She shook her head, fighting for air. Just in case he had moved closer, she frantically waved him away. "I'm—fine…" she wheezed. "Back—off!"

After another few seconds, she began to breathe more normally. Bending to rest her elbows on the counter, she wiped teary eyes. Maybe she would live after all.

"You should sit." She felt warmth engulf her upper arm. A second later she was being tugged away from the counter. Without strength to resist, she allowed herself to be guided. When she felt the brush of a wooden bench against the back of her knees, she sat down heavily. Slumping forward she dropped her head to her hands.

"I'm sorry."

Even as weak and faint as she was, she heard it, but she had trouble believing her ears. Roth Jerric apologizing? She peered at him, unsettled to find that he'd seated himself next to her. She wanted to demand, *What's wrong with the bench on the other side of the table?* but didn't feel up to a brawl at the moment. "I must be delirious. I thought I heard you say you were sorry," she said in a raspy whisper.

"I did."

"Okay, I'll bite," she said. "Sorry for what?"

"For making you choke."

She inhaled for strength. "You should be."

"But that doesn't alter the facts."

Darn her hide for letting him draw her into conversation. But curiosity got the better of her. "What facts?"

"Fact one, that you and I were bathed in that magical light— together. And fact two, we're fated to be lovers."

Such fanciful folderol coming out of Roth Jerric's mouth was too bizarre to be believed. She sat back and glared at him. His eyes sparkled as though he were playing a game—like Cat and Mouse—and she was the mouse. "Funny man." She didn't plan to play mouse to his cat. "Here are the facts as I see them. Fact one, the fate thing was about marriage, not..." Why did she have trouble saying the word lovers? It must be those disturbing, sparkling eyes. "Not...that other thing. Fact two," she hurried on, "I don't, for a second, see you as a believer in Fate."

He was too close for the half grin he aimed her way. His teeth shone, straight and white, and positively wolfish. She quivered at the lewd implications of that expression. "Really?" he asked.

Those eyes were riveting, paralyzing. She couldn't think or move, only stare. A strange combination of fear and anticipation began to sizzle along her nerves, like an unconscious awareness of an approaching lightning storm.

She could feel his energy, dominating the room, hijacking her senses. "Assumptions, Miss Hudson, can be dangerous," he murmured. "You hardly know me."

His hand suddenly cupped the back of her head, drawing her face to his. Hungry, searching lips covered hers. The boldness of his act sang through her veins, his kiss more potent and delicious than she dared admit. He explored, savored, tantalized with his tongue. She tried to steel herself, but too soon began to quiver with the smoldering intensity of the experience.

Never had she known such an instant, impetuous need stir to life deep within her. Shocked by the strength of her arousal, but bewilderingly uncaring, she disregarded the warning bells going off in her head and parted her lips in invitation. Her arms snaking around his shoulders, she leaned in, breast to chest, rubbing boldly, her body's response an explicit yes, pledging to grant his every lusty request.

As surprisingly as it began, his kiss ended. His mouth lifted away, no longer thrilling and enticing. His body no longer touched and tantalized hers. She felt limp, desolate, broken. Her arms slid away to hang loosely at her side. Her lips throbbed and burned.

The pressure of his hand against her head eased, though he didn't quite relinquish his claim. His fingers trailed slowly, deliberately downward, pausing at her nape. "You're right about one thing," he whispered. "I don't believe in Fate." Cunning fingers drifted languidly on, southward along her spine, until his hand came to rest provocatively, just below the small of her back. "But, I love a challenge."

CHAPTER FOUR

"ROTH JERRIC, you are indefensible!" Hannah muttered, slowly recovering from his blitz kiss. Sadly, her recovery was too slow to give him the piece of her mind she belatedly managed to pull together. By the time she came out of her mental blackout, he was gone. Had he said something about a swim? She shook her head. For all she knew he had said he was going to take a stroll on Mars. The truth was, she'd completely lost her mind, so who knew what conceptual problems she might be having, including auditory hallucinations.

She had half a mind to follow him outside and ream him out properly. "How dare he kiss me like that!" *Especially like that,* she added silently. *Why couldn't he have kissed me like he had the lips of a dead fish? Why did he have to kiss me like—like...* What? Who? She'd never been kissed like Roth Jerric kissed her. Well, possibly in a particularly erotic dream, but never for real. She fisted her hands, annoyed with her heated reaction. What did he do, teach kissing?

She pushed herself up from the table. "Okay, okay," she muttered. "You may kiss like a kissing genius, and you may adore a challenge to your heart's content, but *that* was the only kiss you're getting out of me."

She stalked all the way out of the kitchen before she remembered her dirty dishes. How unfair to leave a mess for Joan. The woman had enough work. Heaving a low sigh of frustration, she pivoted around and headed back, making quick work of her dish and glass. Then she remembered Roth's juice tumbler and turned to eye it, torn between cleaning up his mess as a favor to Joan, or leaving it as a symbol of his utter self-centeredness.

The glass wasn't sitting on the table where she last saw it.

"Hmm," she mused aloud. "He can dematerialize objects, too? Idiot Savant Jerric, The Magnificent." Getting more upset by the second, she wondered if she'd been locked in her stupor longer than she realized? Had he left the table, washed, dried and put away his glass, then exited the house for his jog around Mars, or his swim—whichever—and she'd been too blindsided by his kiss to notice?

She moaned at the thought and slumped against the counter. He must be having a great laugh at her expense, having seen her motionless as a post, glassy-eyed, staring into space. Then again, maybe he got reactions like that from a lot of women. She'd heard rumors about his popularity with the female sex. Lots of them. Different and varied types, temporary playthings. Maybe messing with a woman's mind—and *lips*—was his hobby. Maybe he blitzed handy, random women with his sultry kisses, and their heated reactions were no more titillating for him than finishing a picture puzzle. Satisfying, yes, but neither amusing nor arousing.

Still, the thought that he managed to make her react so warmly to the caress of his lips tore at her. She didn't want her effect on him to be satisfaction. She wanted to make him feel below par, in a word—mediocre.

With an angry flourish she tossed the dish cloth over the towel bar. She had no confidence that she held the power to make him feel mediocre, but she certainly held the power *not* to give him any more gratification at her expense. "Find some other challenge, because, kissing genius or no kissing genius, you're not turning me into your picture puzzle again." She wasn't sure that made sense, but considering how late it was, she decided to blame it on fatigue. Cinching her robe tight, she marched out of the kitchen and up the stairs to her bedroom.

She climbed into bed and curled into an unhappy ball. Never before had she hoped not to have an erotic dream. Tonight she hoped fervently to dream of things mundane and forgettable. Nothing erotic, nothing sexy. If something hot and sensual were to slip into her dreams, she feared she knew who would be a major participant, and she didn't need Roth Jerric tromping through her dream world, too.

Roth skimmed the dark surface of the cove, swimming as though chased by sharks. He swam with the energy of a man furious with himself and taking it out on his body. He knew that tiring himself out like this, in cold, black water lit only by moonlight, would cool the fire Hannah's kiss ignited in his belly.

Swimming alone, especially at night, in the dark, where any motorboat might speed across his path and cut him to ribbons, was not wise. But why break a streak of stupidity now? Why in all that was holy had he kissed Hannah Hudson? She annoyed the fire out of him. Especially after he heard her spout off about how loathsome he was. Loathsome? What in Hades had he done to her but pay her a respectable living wage?

Deciding he'd pressed his luck as far as he dared, he flipped around and headed toward shore. Maybe now he could sleep, having tired himself out with his mad, dead-of-night race. He reached shallow water and stood, trudging the rest of the way to shore. Flinging dripping hair from his eyes, he stared up at the inn. Her light was out. Good. He had no desire to run into her on his way to bed. He'd just owe her another apology. Maybe two, since he apparently couldn't keep his hands off her.

He checked his watch. She still had five minutes of bathroom time before the clock struck one. Okay, fine. He'd make sure she was good and done before he went inside. When he hit shore he collapsed on his back in the grass, breathing hard. Lacing his fingers behind his head, he stared up at the night sky. Stars twinkled peacefully, as though the havoc of his day had no effect on them. He managed a wry grin. Of course not. The world still spun and the heavens still promised quiet, starry views, gentle moonlight and cool night breezes, no matter how foolish one elderly woman was about her financial troubles, or how revolted one young woman might be at the sight of him.

His smile died. "And you kissed her, you fool," he muttered. "You revolt her, but you kissed her." He closed his eyes, trying to erase the memory. But even with the smell of lake water in his nostrils, her scent lingered—reminiscent of honeysuckle and sunshine.

He snorted, disgusted with himself. "Don't you have enough on your plate, Jerric?" he asked. What was all that bull hockey about loving a challenge? He did, of course. But why suggest he planned to seduce her? The thought had never entered his head. At least not in any conscious way. But suddenly he was spouting off about loving a challenge, as though the kiss was only round one in his seduction strategy.

"You're trying to regain your zest for life, Jerric, not hook up with some virtual stranger for a meaningless romp between the sheets." He crossed his legs at the ankles. "Or in the grass," he added. An image of making love to Hannah out here on a soft, summer evening like this one, filled his mind. He clamped his jaws, annoyed with himself. With an explosive blasphemy, he pushed up to sit. "Get a grip," he ground out. "She loathes you, and after tonight, she'll avoid you like a flu epidemic. Besides, you have this lake property to acquire. *Focus.* Remember why you came here."

He stood up, once again scanning the sky in all its peaceful vastness. He wished he could reach up, grab a handful of the cosmic calm and take it inside himself. "Kissing Hannah Hudson isn't a smart way to find inner serenity," he muttered. Shaking his head at his unexplainable lapse, he headed toward the inn, looking forward to a shower and the restful detachment of sleep.

Dreamless sleep.

The Fourth of July fell on a Tuesday. Not that it mattered to Hannah, being jobless. She simply marked it on her calendar, more as a matter of course than to earmark the national holiday. To her it was simply one more day of semi-success avoiding Roth Jerric. Ever since the kiss in the kitchen, she pointedly refused to speak to him at meals. Didn't even look in his direction. Well, most of the time she didn't. Every so often she became aware of something he was doing, like smiling at Joan, his cheek dimple sending spiraling currents of—of something she didn't care to name cascading along her spine. Furious with herself that she couldn't keep her promise to dismiss him with a vengeance, she quickly swung her attention elsewhere.

This evening, ignoring Roth should have been easy, since an attractive male guest joined them for supper. The sheriff, Deacon Vance, in his crisp brown uniform, arrived around seven, to eat and to watch the fireworks display in Grove, twelve miles away. The best view, Joan announced, was from the balconies off Hannah's and Roth's rooms.

Hannah was secretly glad she'd picked up her things. She didn't like the idea of Deacon or Roth traipsing through her room with lacy underthings strewn about. One positive result coming from her attempts to avoid Roth was the free time she had to find mindless activities. One of which had been straightening up her room. She spent restless energy dusting, which hadn't been a bad idea. Poor Joan had clearly become too arthritic to reach the ceiling fan blades. Hannah discovered they were coated with years of dust. The accumulation cascaded down on her, making her go into a sneezing spasm that nearly launched her off her chair.

That dirt, grime and near broken neck when she almost fell

were only memories. How sad that neither Deacon nor Roth, both over six feet tall, were quite gigantic enough to discover how sparkling clean the top of the fan blades were.

She heard her name and looked up from her supper of chicken fried steak, mashed potatoes and fresh green beans. She'd been so immersed in thought she had lost the thread of conversation. Swallowing, she glanced around, attempting to figure out who had spoken to her. Though she made it a point not to look at Roth, everyone else's attention was trained on her. She feared he stared at her, too. With an apologetic smile, she gave up her pretense that she'd been listening and said to no one in particular, "I'm sorry. What?"

"I asked about your family," the sheriff said with a charming grin. My, but he was attractive, lean and muscular, clean-shaven, with an honest, engaging face. From the way he filled out his uniform, she could tell his physique was nicely proportioned and he was in great shape. She supposed law-and-order types needed to keep physically fit, in case they had to run after a culprit and wrestle him into submission.

Deacon Vance looked like he could wrestle anybody into submission. His dark brown eyes echoed the color of his hair. Then there was that smile, radiating a real, down-home friendliness impossible not to return in kind.

She smiled, meaning it. "Oh, I'm an only child." Her smile dimmed. "My folks are divorced."

Vance's expression grew serious. "I'm sorry."

"It wasn't your fault." With only a slight pang at the memory, she managed to regain her happy expression.

"But it must be tough."

"I was grown up." She shrugged. "But it taught me one thing."

"Really?" Vance asked. "What was that?"

"Not to depend on a man for anything." She stopped smiling. This was a serious area for her.

His forehead creased. "I hope the experience hasn't soured your opinion of men."

She felt Roth's eyes drill into her and stifled a shiver of awareness. "Not—altogether," she said, a tad more grimly than she meant to. "Just the overbearing, self-satisfied, condescending types." *Take that, Roth Jerric.*

Deacon's expression grew analytical, though his grin was once again charming. "I can see you've thought this out."

Her smile was a reflexive response. "Oh, yes—especially lately."

"Well, aren't you two getting along famously," Joan chimed in, sounding delighted. "But we need to finish our supper in the next ten minutes. Fireworks will be starting. We'll have dessert after." She paused, patted her lips with her napkin. "I've made my yummy Red, White and Blue apple pandowdy."

"And it is yummy." Deacon aimed a friendly flash of teeth at his hostess. "It wouldn't be the Fourth without Joan Peterson's pandowdy."

Hannah was once again drawn in by the sheriff's smile. Her feminine intuition told her his interest in her went beyond polite dinner conversation. She wasn't sure how she felt about that. His good looks were enough to attract any sane woman. And he was obviously an upright citizen. Not necessarily because he was a sheriff, since small-town corruption in government officials wasn't unheard-of, but because Joan Peterson valued his friendship.

Hannah knew Joan well enough by now to be sure of her keen sense about people. Because she'd been friends with Deacon Vance for years, she would know his character. And since he was here, an invited guest, his character must be as uncorrupted as Mrs. Peterson's devotion to her husband's memory and to her home.

Forcing her gaze away from Deacon's hypnotic smile, she attempted to finish her meal. "The chicken fried steak is wonderful," she said, slicing off a bite.

"Why, thank you, dear."

"It is," Roth said. "I don't think I've ever had better."

Hannah's attention remained steadfastly on her plate, though the urge to peep at Roth nagged.

"She's the best cook around," Deacon said, then finished off his iced tea with a clink of ice. "Why do you think I let her speed all over creation and never give her a ticket." He winked at Hannah, and she had trouble swallowing.

"Deke, you're such a tease." Joan giggled. "You know I never even bend the law."

Deacon made a show of looking thunderstruck, charmingly so. "Listen to the woman's flimflamming. I've clocked her going eighty in a twenty-five-mile-an-hour zone. If it weren't for the fact that she bribes me with her delicious meals, she'd be in the calaboose right now."

Joan blushed like a schoolgirl. "Silly boy. He's always teasing me. My poor old car can't even go over thirty miles an hour." She wagged a finger at him. "Now, stop being a naughty sheriff and finish your meal. We don't want to miss those fireworks."

"Yes, 'um," he said, with all the charisma of an unrepentant charmer. His laughing gaze cruised from Joan, at the far end of the table, to Hannah, around the corner to his left. Oh, yes, her intuition was dead on. Deacon Vance was definitely flirting.

Hannah lowered her gaze to her food, in a quandary over how to respond. She was free to flirt back, so why the hesitance to smile coyly and bat her lashes at him? He was big, strong, handsome and witty, a person of good character, and clearly interested.

What was her problem? A voice in her head started to answer, but she blocked it with a noisy cough.

"Are you all right, dear?" Joan asked.

Hannah cleared her throat. "Um—fine." She motioned toward her neck. "A little gravy down the wrong pipe." She took a sip of iced tea, inwardly scolding the little voice, demanding that it keep its meddling mouth shut.

"Well, ladies and gentlemen…" Joan placed her napkin beside her plate and nodded encouragingly at her guests. "Shall we go watch the fireworks?"

Roth took a spot between his balcony door and Hannah's, and leaned against the wood siding with its flaky peeling surface. The others in attendance stood at the metal rail, oohing and aahing over the dramatic display, twice as dramatic due to its reflection on the lake.

Roth pursed his lips, his regard drawn away from the exploding pinwheels in the sky, to Hannah's back, and the way her body seemed to skew ever so slightly toward the grinning ape of a sheriff.

And the way his big paw and her hand grazed one another as they clutched the rail. He crossed his arms and snorted derisively.

"What?" Joan asked, turning. "Did you say something Ross?"

He didn't look her way, his gaze dwelling on the little drama of the teasing hands. "Not a thing," he murmured.

"You don't look like you're enjoying the fireworks," Joan said. "Why don't you come out here to the rail."

He smirked. Like being three feet closer made a difference. "I'm fine."

"But you're not even looking up," she went on. "You're looking at Hannah's bottom."

This time he did look up, astonished by the woman's audacity, however inaccurate her observation—at least for the moment. It wasn't like Hannah's backside was something to be ignored. Those hips of hers were certainly a ripe little package. Still, in his defense, at that precise moment he had *not* been engrossed in the moonlit view of her posterior.

Both Hannah and Deacon turned. The sheriff looked dubious and possibly slightly amused. Hannah looked cautiously unsure, as though she didn't think she'd heard right. Mona paid no heed, bless her creative oblivion. Suddenly thrown in the spotlight, an accusation hanging in the air, Roth felt strangely guilty and self-conscious. He couldn't recall feeling this vulnerable and conflicted, at least not since the onset of puberty.

Damn it. He was no adolescent now. He was a grown man being accused of—if not quite literally caught—ogling a woman's backside. So what? What the hell was criminal about that? Just because she didn't like him didn't detract from the nicely packed pair of jeans she wore.

With a wry grin, he said without apology, "I'm a man and she's got a nice tush. So sue me." He angled his crooked grin at Hannah, her expression now a most alluring picture of wide-eyed hostility. Joan's face showed plain, unadulterated horror, while Deacon merely raised an eyebrow in a wordless, one-man-to-another challenge, *Why in blazes dig yourself into a deeper hole by admitting it, ol' buddy?*

Damned if he knew. He shrugged but his indifference was a sham. He lifted his attention to the fireworks display. Rather than enjoy the incandescent extravaganza in the sky, all his mind's eye pictured was the scorching inferno in Hannah's stare.

"So, you had a good time last night?"

Hannah was brought up short by Joan's question. She turned away from peeling potatoes for their midday meal. She'd begun to assist Joan with chores, not so much out of guilt for getting the free stay, but because she had grown to care for the elderly woman and wanted to help her. "Last night?" she asked, absently. Her thoughts, she feared, had wandered to Roth and his unvarnished interest in her "tush."

She wished he hadn't made that remark, because it set off unruly and very unwelcome desire alarms. How bizarre! How delinquent and wrong! And so unlike her. Usually she had better control over her instincts and emotions. Usually she didn't harbor lusty feelings for unworthy men, especially those who found her wanting. Correction. Had she already forgotten Milo? And now she felt carnal pangs for the thoroughly contemptible Roth Jerric? She had to make another correction. Apparently he didn't find her tush wanting. But as for the rest of her…

She closed her eyes, attempting to squelch thoughts of Roth. Joan's remark clearly referred to Deacon, a darling man who deserved hot, earthy thoughts. Why was she wasting them on a man so undeserving?

With difficulty, she managed a smile for her hostess. "Yes, last night was—very memorable."

Joan smiled and sighed as though reassured. "I was sure of it." She squeezed Hannah's hand holding the half-peeled potato, leaving a film of flour, residue of pie-crust preparation. "Perhaps the phenomenon of the blue moon doesn't always dictate a couple's fate, after all."

"I certainly hope not," Hannah said, more to herself than to Joan. "The notion that Mr. Roth-Self-Important-Condescending-Jerric and I are fated to be soul mates is so ridiculous it's laughable." She began to peel the potato with renewed zeal.

"Then you really like Deacon?"

"Really." She peeled faster and faster, wishing she were absolutely crazy about Deacon Vance. He deserved to be admired and appreciated. Tragically widowed when his young bride of only six months, a bank teller, was shot to death in a robbery. That tragedy, Joan had told Hannah, was the driving force for Deacon's turn from construction work to law enforcement.

Since his wife's death, eight years before, he'd thrown himself into his work, dating rarely. He became quite the local hero, and though the matrons of Delaware county continually threw their daughters and granddaughters his way, he evidently had not yet relinquished his devotion for his lost love. But according to Joan's chatter this morning, Deacon was unusually chipper and attentive last night. Joan was thrilled.

Hannah felt guilty and was angry with herself. Why this attraction, lately, for men who were not only no good for her, but were shallow, domineering jerks?

"Oh, dear." Placing a hand on the younger woman's, Joan halted Hannah's peeling frenzy. "That's not a potato anymore, dear. It's a pea." She laughed. "I shouldn't have reminded you of Deacon. Obviously the memory energizes you."

Hannah wanted to correct her hostess, not build up her hopes. She feared with Roth around she wouldn't be able to give Deacon the attention he deserved. Her radar for good guys was getting a lot of unwanted static. But Joan's elation kept her from speaking. Maybe, with effort, she could redirect her radar for better, non-staticky performance, and then she'd be able to appreciate Deacon Vance for the great guy he was. "The sheriff is one of the best looking, nicest men I've met in a long time," she admitted. "Roth Jerric is arrogant, pushy and greedy. He can't hold a candle to Deacon, so that blue moon thing is *hardly* foolproof."

"Am I interrupting?"

Roth's voice jarred Hannah. Not because it wasn't melodious and sexy, because it was. Too melodious and sexy. No, it jarred her because she'd just savaged him again, and he must have overheard.

"Why, no, dear boy." Joan sounded bubbly, no doubt due to Hannah's assessment of Deacon versus Roth. Her antagonism toward the man who threatened to take away her home, it appeared, had taken a back seat to her cheerfulness over what was shaping up to look suspiciously like matchmaking. "Hannah and I were simply chitchatting."

"Yes, I heard." He sounded as though he might be weary of hearing himself disparaged so often and openly. "Don't mind me," he went on. "I'm just getting a cup of coffee for Mona. The urn is empty."

"I poured out the last of what was left, but I've brewed a fresh pot." Joan smiled at him. "It's thoughtful of you to do that for Mona."

He didn't respond, but went to the coffeepot and filled the mug he carried. After replacing the carafe on the warming plate, he glanced at the women. Or more pointedly, at Hannah. "Good morning," he said with a nonchalant nod, as though he wasn't churning with annoyance over her outspoken contempt.

He either had a very thick hide or he didn't care what she thought. That idea smarted. He *should* care. If the world were fair, her low opinion of him should cause him the same degree of obsessive agitation as his insultingly broadcast appreciation for her backside—a remark she couldn't seem to properly forget.

Now she was the one churning with annoyance. With a stiff nod in return, she said, "It was a good morning." She paused for effect. "Until recently." She made a show of turning away and plucking up another potato. She set to work, the peelings sailing helter skelter across the counter top, entirely missing a large bowl, their intended target.

"How ironic," he said to her back. "The day just took a major upturn for me."

She heard his footfalls grow faint and knew when he left the kitchen. Frowning now, she stopped peeling. What exactly did he mean by "major upturn?" Was it the reassurance that his presence darkened her day that caused his day to brighten? Or could it have been another veiled crack about her backside? Now she wished she hadn't decided to wear shorts that were quite so short and formfitting. Whichever way he meant "major upturn," her hands itched to slap him. At least that's what she prayed her hands itched to do to him.

CHAPTER FIVE

HANNAH had never been more than a tolerable painter, but considering Joan's arthritis, she knew she could do a better job painting the central hallway than her hostess. So, after breakfast, when Joan dragged out the paint-smeared gallon can, Hannah shooed her away and insisted on doing the job.

The trouble was filling the nail holes left by artwork of Mona's and former visiting, resident artists. Joan didn't have all the necessary equipment, so without a putty knife, Hannah was reduced to daubing spackling compound into holes with her finger, then smoothing it out with the back side of a pink comb she fished out of her handbag. It wasn't a bad job, but it wasn't all that good, either.

She checked her watch. Nine-thirty. The compound would be dry enough to paint by now. With the prying end of a hammer, she began to force open the can of off-white paint.

"What are you doing?"

The voice was uncomfortably familiar. She didn't look up at Roth, but kept working on opening the can. "I'm composing an operetta. What does it look like?"

"Not much like that," he said.

She could hear his footfalls over the scattered newspaper. Why was he coming toward her? That's all she needed. Mr. Perfect coming to criticize her work.

"What are all the lumps on the walls?"

She peered at him. "Lumps?"

He stopped nearby to tower above her as she squatted beside the paint can. He indicated one of her filled holes. "Lumps," he repeated.

"That's not a lump," she said. "It's perfectly flat. It just looks like a lump because it's lighter than the wall. It's an optical illusion." She wasn't sure she totally believed that herself, but she didn't appreciate her careful handiwork being referred to as lumpy.

He ran a hand over the filled hole. "It's not bad, but it needs sanding. Otherwise it will look lumpy once it's painted."

She heaved a weighty sigh to indicate her aggravation. "Look, nobody enjoys your criticism more than I do, but it doesn't look lumpy to me." She thought about admitting she was a little short on painter's tools, but decided against it. He'd probably find her pink comb solution not only hilarious, but stupid. She didn't need him laughing at her right now. "Besides," she added, "once I put back the artwork, any—" she refused to use the word "lumps" "—any *slight* variations won't be visible, because they'll be hidden behind the pictures."

He raised an eyebrow, looking skeptical. As though a half-assed job, no matter what the excuse, was still half-assed. She didn't like the feeling that look gave her. It fairly screamed "mediocre." In her own defense, she gritted out, "Joan didn't have any sandpaper. Just this putty and the paint."

He nodded as though that didn't surprise him. "There are a lot of things she needs that she doesn't have." His jaw muscles flexed as though he gritted his teeth. After a second, he indicated the can. "Don't open that yet. I have an idea."

"What are you going to do?" she asked, feeling sarcastic. "*Make* me some sandpaper?"

"Just wait," he said. With a quick wink that almost knocked Hannah back on her posterior, he turned and walked around the corner toward the kitchen.

She crouched there, staring after him, her mouth open. When she recovered, she made a sour face. "The wall is not lumpy." She went back to prying open the can, annoyed by his assessment of her work. "I should be used to your disapproval by now," she muttered. "I can't help it if my only tool is a plastic comb. I suppose I should apologize for not carrying around sheets of sandpaper along with my wallet and lipstick." With a creak, the lid popped free. She judiciously removed it to the newspaper covered floor avoiding getting any paint on herself, then picked up the stirring stick.

As she stirred, she surveyed the walls from her squatted vantage point. She did notice slight—make that very, *very* minute—variations in the wall's surface where she'd combed the compound. "Only a control freak would notice," she mumbled.

Approaching footfalls alerted her to the fact that Roth was returning. Was that possible? How could he have made sandpaper in five minutes? More likely he kept various grades of it stowed in his car trunk for little one-upmanship-perfectionism situations like this. She gritted her teeth.

"Here you go." He rounded the corner from the kitchen. When he reached her he held out his hand.

She eyed his fingers, which seemed to be wadding or crushing something green. It didn't look much like a sheet of sandpaper.

She eyed him, full of mistrust, then stood. Though still woefully short for a nose-to-nose confrontation, she felt more in control on her feet. When she didn't reach for his offering, he opened his hand. A crumpled, wiry shoot of some plant lay there. She lifted her focus from the mangled sprig to his face. "Why are you shoving weeds at me?"

"It's homemade sandpaper."

When she still didn't reach for it, he shook his head. "Okay, I'll prove it." He walked to the wall and began to brush the weed lightly back and forth over one of her putty jobs. Surprisingly, after only a few strokes, the bulge disappeared. He moved on to the next one, giving her the space she preferred to better inspect the one he had recently filed down. Running a finger across it, she had to admit, it did look good.

She experienced a rush of resentment, hating the idea of conceding he was not only right about the lumps, but that he could conjure up sandpaper out of what looked like porch sweepings. The notion galled her that he was superior to her in any way, in even such a mundane activity as prepainting preparations.

She feared she might have to say something nice in a minute, so to vent her spleen she silently cursed him up one side and down the other without spewing out the words that hovered on her tongue. Even so, she couldn't quite hold back a low, hissing exhale.

He shifted to look at her. "Did you say something?"

She watched him as he sanded away a fourth lump. "Nope." She shoved her hands into her jeans hip pockets, stubbornly refusing to compliment him.

He watched her for another beat, then turned back to his work. "You can start painting. I'll finish sanding."

"Whatever." She clamped her mouth shut. She would not say thank you to this man for proving her wrong. No way! No how! She hunkered down to finish stirring. She knew exactly where he was by the slight rasping sound of his work. After a few more minutes, when she decided the paint was stirred enough, she picked up her brush and dipped it in. "Okay, okay," she said, unable to beat back her curiosity any longer. "What is that stuff?"

He didn't respond. She couldn't even hear him sanding. Where was he and what was he doing? Puzzled, she turned to look behind her, felt resistance in her brush hand, then realized too late that he had moved across the hallway and was very close. So close, in fact, that her paintbrush had just slapped a sloppy off-white strip across the chest of his navy polo shirt.

"Oh!" She yanked the brush away. Unfortunately her reflexive recoil was to clutch the brush to her breast. "Oh!" Wet, sticky paint soaked through her cotton T-shirt. She grimaced, feeling like a complete nitwit.

Ever since he had walked into the hallway she'd made one stupid mistake after another. First, she'd been too prideful to thank him for his help. Then her curiosity, mixed with her nervousness, had ruined his designer shirt which must have cost close to a hundred bucks. And lastly, she had clasped a paint-soaked brush to her breast like some old movie slap-stick stooge.

Forcing herself to look at him, she said earnestly, "I'm so sorry."

He appeared less upset than startled. His glance moved from his shirtfront to hers, then to her face. She was glad she couldn't read minds. No doubt he was thinking she was the biggest flake on earth. Swallowing, she said, "If you put your ear up really close to mine, people tell me you can hear the ocean." She bit her lip. Why was she calling herself dumb? To this man of all men! Another moronic mouth overload to add to a mounting list.

His brow crinkled, then his lips parted in a crooked grin. "Okay." Surprising her, he bent enough to place his ear close to hers. She was so stunned, she couldn't move. What was the man going to do, rub her nose in it?

"I don't hear a thing," he said softly.

Reflexively she turned and found herself practically mouth-to-mouth with him, their lips a mere inch apart.

His eyes flickered with an appealing warmth. She watched those eyes for as long as she dared, breaking eye contact with difficulty. Despite her effort to appear poised, she could feel herself shaking. "I—was kidding." She shifted away, hoping she was kidding, though she still felt like the world's biggest fool.

And she probably looked it, a dripping paintbrush crushed

against her chest. She didn't dare remove it for fear the wet fabric sticking to her would reveal that she'd opted to go braless for the hot work. The air-conditioning didn't perform very well at its best, and was off now. Windows were thrown open to help dissipate paint fumes. So far, all she'd managed to paint were Roth's chest and hers.

"Good," he said.

She wasn't sure what he meant.

"It's horsetail."

"What?" Now she was totally confused. Against her better judgment she faced him, still too near for her peace of mind. He watched her with a speculative expression, not quite amused but on the brink. Why did she feel light-headed and weak-kneed? She feared the paint fumes were getting to her. Otherwise how could she explain a sudden, demented urge to lift her lips to his for an encore of that intoxicating kiss she couldn't quite forget?

"Are you all right?" His breath teased her lips.

She nodded absently. It was a lie. She was far from all right.

"You look flushed." She felt his hand at her elbow. "Maybe you should sit. Let me have that."

She felt him tug on the paintbrush and resisted. "No!"

"Why? It's ruining your shirt."

"It's fine," she said. It came out an octave too high.

"Don't be silly." He tugged.

She yanked with all her strength. "Stop that! I don't have a bra on!" She dug her teeth into her lower lip. If she drew blood that would be dandy. She deserved to bleed for blurting that out.

"Oh," he said. "Sorry." He let go of her hand, but the warmth of his skin lingered. "Sit down." His hand on her elbow, she felt herself being urged to the newspapered floor.

"Please, I'm fine. I'm just—just upset," she admitted. "I ruined your shirt. I'll pay for it."

"It's an old shirt."

She avoided his eyes, seeing nothing as she sat cross-legged. "Just leave. I can finish sanding."

"Aren't you going to change?"

"Why should I? It won't hurt this top if I get more paint on it now." She glanced at him from beneath her lashes. He knelt on one knee, looking ridiculously yummy. The fresh painted strip on his shirt somehow managed to make his chest look broader. And because it stuck to him a bit, his pectoral muscles were a little too obvious for her peace of mind.

"I thought you were embarrassed because your top is wet—"

"If you go away, there won't be any problem, will there?"

He started to speak, then looking solemn, nodded. "I see your point." With that he stood. "I'll just finish sanding."

"Don't…" she said, a pleading edge in her tone. She worked to lose it. "Just—go."

He frowned slightly, as though he would like to argue the point. But after a second, he bent toward her and stretched out his hand. "Here."

This time she offered one of her paint-streaked hands, wishing she'd taken the dratted ball of weeds in the first place. "Thanks," she murmured.

Rather than drop the green wad into her palm, he turned his hand over, lay it there, closing his fingers around hers. "It's horsetail," he said softly. "It owes its roughness to being rich in silica. When crumpled it scours like fine-texture sandpaper. Dad and I used it for sandpaper when I was a kid." He continued to hold her hand as he spoke. "This should be enough to finish the hall."

She heard him, but her main focus was on his fingers, enfolding hers. Her heart beat, hard and fast, beneath the paintbrush she clutched. *Let go of my hand,* she demanded silently, not really wanting him to. What was wrong with her? *Let it be the paint fumes,* she prayed, squeezing her eyes shut.

Somehow, with the visual disconnect, she managed to pull her fingers from his. "Please…go," she whispered.

Silence stretched out for a painfully long interlude before he said, "Right." A couple of seconds ticked by before he added, "No problem." Somehow she sensed it was a bit of a problem for him. Could it be that he didn't want to leave her? She shook off the odd notion. It had to be the paint fumes, affecting her mind.

She heard movement as he stood up, heard his footsteps as he walked away across the newspaper and bounded up the stairs. After a few more minutes, she was able to open her eyes. Gingerly she pulled the soggy brush off her T-shirt. Depositing the ball of horsetail on the floor, she picked the sticky, wet fabric away from her breasts. "Thank goodness for latex paint," she muttered. Laying the brush across the paint can, she retrieved the ball of horsehair weed. It felt warm. She wished it didn't, because she knew whose warmth it retained. "Even a stupid weed has trouble getting you completely out of its system," she whispered sadly.

What a shock, Hannah thought, disconcerted to see Deacon Vance's sheriff's car on the gravel parking area at the side of the inn. She leaned on the balcony railing, wondering what convoluted ploy Joan had used today to get her prospective soul mate out to the inn. Yesterday, at seven, she had just showered and changed after painting the hallway when Deacon arrived in answer to Joan's frantic call for help. The dire threat had been a pack of marauding wolves that turned out to be a mother deer and her two fawns grazing in the nearby woods. Since it was suppertime, Deacon had, of course, been included.

What make-believe catastrophe was on today's agenda? An ax murderer in the form of an inadvertently trespassing fisherman? An escaped tiger in the garden that would turn out to be somebody's roaming cat?

She looked at her watch. Not quite seven o'clock in the morning. Whatever excuse Joan had used to lure him here, Hannah felt sure Deacon would be invited to join them for breakfast. She decided she'd better get out of her robe and into something cool. Already the day showed signs of muggy heat. Even in her lightweight cotton robe with nothing on underneath but panties and a bra, she began to feel sticky from the high humidity.

She turned, then immediately stilled, startled to discover Roth watching her. He wore nothing but navy boxers and leaned against the jamb of his open patio door. How casually sexy he looked there with his arms crossed loosely over his flat stomach.

He inclined his head. "Morning."

She swallowed, blinked, but could manage nothing more. How long had he been there, silently observing her.

He cocked his head toward the parking area. "I see the Lone Ranger is back." He pursed his lips. "How's the romance going?"

Even though Hannah felt Joan's matchmaking had little chance of success, she decided Roth's remark was too cynical to let pass unchallenged. "Jealous?" Astounded at her own question, she blanched. Where had *that* come from? She'd meant to say, "Just dandy!"

With a flexing of arm and chest muscles, he pushed away from the door and walked out of the shade, suddenly all sunlit and golden. The sight stole her breath. "Yes," he said, his voice husky and soft.

She experienced an unexpected thrill. For once he didn't seem to be mocking her. No matter how golden and sexy he looked, she had enough rational discipline to back away, which wasn't much help since mere inches brought her hard against the balcony rail.

"I don't want to be jealous," he went on.

She felt a curious, cascading pull in the pit of her stomach. His eyes, a striking blue, seemed to be making passionate promises.

"I didn't come here for a fling," he whispered.

She winced, unsure why. He was so near. She inhaled his scent and felt pleasantly drugged by his clean, fresh-from-the-shower aroma. All she could be sure of was that he took hold of her arms, not harshly, but with definite intent. His eyes gleamed, beckoned; his lips gravitated downward. "You provoke me—" his mouth brushed hers, goading, taunting "—to the point of losing control." His lips were surprisingly soft and sensitive as they took possession of her mouth.

Oh, those lips. The barest touch seemed to have the power to extinguish her good sense. Some small voice inside her brain balked, shouted out bits and pieces of a vow, swearing the only kiss he would ever get from her...what? The words grew jumbled in her head, didn't fit together. All she could fully appreciate was the earth-shattering caress of those clever lips.

She felt his skin, warm beneath her fingertips and realized she had slid her arms about his waist. His hands were on the move, too. One slid up to cup her head while the other slid to her back, then southward, closing intimately over her bottom. She shivered with his bold familiarity, yet nothing about the act set off alarms. She no longer heard the warning voice in her head, experienced no desire to be rescued from the gentle cordon of his arms.

Her hands skidded over the muscles of his back. She relished his hard, male texture. The magic of his mouth and his seductive touch set her aflame. She opened her lips and their kiss deepened. Their tongues flicked, teased, languidly entwined. Nothing could have prepared her for such poignant, aching bliss.

She heard him groan. He lifted his lips slightly, whispering, "Come inside."

An instant later she felt herself being drawn forward, half aware of what was happening. It became darker, cooler. She blinked, trying to put to rights both her vision and her sluggish brain. She felt herself being lifted from the ground and gasped with the loss of her footing.

A deep chuckle filled her head and tingled through her breasts. "We're just changing locations," he whispered, close to her ear. "It was too public out there."

She watched him in a half-dream state. He smiled and she smiled back. He had such an irresistible smile—and those dimples...

She found herself lowered to his bed. He leaned over her, caressed her cheek. She inhaled his scent, thoroughly delicious, as was the brush of his hand against her jaw, her throat. His eyes, framed by thick, ebony lashes, glowed with desire. She experienced a heady rush of gratification at the sight.

"Better than breakfast..." he murmured. His lips settled on hers once more with a lusty, provocative urgency.

Better than breakfast? What did that mean? Something in her brain clicked back on. What was better than breakfast? Was he referring to—*sex?*

As her brain scrambled around for clarity his warm lips caressed her temple. One of his talented hands trailed from her waist to cup her bottom.

Was he suggesting they were about to miss breakfast because they were going to have sex? "Oh..." Her passion-drenched moan was edged with dismay. *Hannah Hudson, what are you doing?* She didn't like the answer stumbling to the forefront of her mind. It seemed to suggest things that would not have been possible an hour ago, even in her wildest, most bizarre dreams.

But was she in his bed? Were his lips on hers? Were his hands dipping into private, intimate places they should not be without a very explicit invitation? Sadly the answers were all very definite yeses. Yeses? She quivered, disconcerted. The fact that she could so easily be aroused by someone she abhorred jolted her back into a tenuous state of rationality. Her brain began to churn out images of what she was on the brink of doing.

"Don't," she breathed, but the sound she made was no more than a sigh. She was so weak, so...so...ready. *But not with him! This is Roth Jerric!* She admonished inwardly. *Don't give him the satisfaction of stomping on your self-confidence, then seducing you! How irrational is that?*

"Don't!" She pressed against his chest, her trembling arms finally taking cues from her brain again. "Stop!"

He laughed, the deep, rich sound awash with innuendo. "Don't worry, sweetheart. I won't." He shifted his hips, pressing himself against her. The sensations brought on an explosive response. The man was as remorselessly charismatic as he was sexually adept.

Full blown insight returned, like the quick, cutting slash of a whip. "No!" She moaned, pressing harder. "Let me go." She shoved out of his embrace and scrambled to sit up. Her limbs were shaky, her breathing shallow. "Just like a man," she cried, her voice low and raw. "How can you want…" She swept the bed with a broad motion. *"This?"* She swallowed to remove the tremor from her voice. "From *me?*"

He drew up on one elbow, his brow crinkling, though his crooked smile remained intact. "You're sexy and beautiful."

She burned from the ends of her hair to the tips of her deep pink toenails. She knew she must be blushing all over, both out of embarrassment for her crazed weakness, and her dim view of him and his whole gender's sexual insincerity. "Nothing else matters?" she asked in disbelief.

His smile dimmed. "What else should?"

Shocked by his bluntness, she gasped. "How can you be so shameless?"

"Shameless?" He looked skeptical. "For calling you sexy and beautiful?"

"No!" How dare he think the fact that he had called her a mediocre employee should make no difference. "How can men compartmentalize these things? If I make love to a man, I have to admire the whole man, not just…" She shook her head, deciding a lecture on ethics would do no good. "I guess your standards crumble when you're horny, huh?"

"*My* standards?" Except for the sharp edge to his question he sounded almost amused. "You have no room to talk when it comes to crumbling standards."

She slid off the bed, then cut her gaze back to him. He watched her and his face held precious little humor.

"What do you mean?"

"I was under the impression you loathed me," he said, nostrils flaring. "But you were turned on, too, sweetheart."

Ouch! At the moment, she might not be in the best position to throw stones. But in her favor, ultimately, she took the higher moral ground. "At least I put a stop to it before it was too late." She cinched her robe so tight she had to stifle a groan of pain. Spinning away, she headed toward the hallway door. With her hand on the knob, she realized darting out of Roth's room, clad so scantily, might give casual observers the wrong idea. Well, maybe not altogether wrong, but very wrong in the sense that anything *really* happened.

She spun around. With her chin angled high, she avoided looking his way and darted to the bathroom door. "I don't care what time it is," she said. "I'm taking a shower. Is that clear?" She didn't wait for his response. A few minutes later she trembled in the tub, scrubbing away all signs of him. How tragic that she couldn't abolish the memory of her near-surrender as easily as she could scrub away his aroma.

When Hannah arrived at breakfast, Roth was already there. And so was Deacon. She'd completely forgotten about him. She felt wicked and guilty and strangely giddy.

"Well, good morning, Miss Hug-a-bed," Joan said pleasantly. "We thought you weren't joining us today."

Hannah slipped into her seat beside Roth. His scent filled her head, making all her unwanted erotic memories come crashing in like a powerful ocean wave, flooding every nook and cranny of her brain. Valiantly she fought the visions, smiling, first at Joan, then Mona and finally Deacon. *Don't feel guilty, she told herself. You were not cheating on anybody. You were simply being extraordinarily stupid. On the other hand, guilt might be a perfectly proper emotion for being so crazed. After all, Roth was right. You do loathe him. How could you have come so close to letting yourself—*

"Good morning," Deacon said, pulling her from her self-re-crimination. Did he have a curious, cop look in his eyes? Did he guess? Could he know? Could Roth have come downstairs and blabbed. *No, no, don't be ridiculous,* she convinced herself silently. *First, even he wouldn't be such a weasel. Second, if he had announced to the breakfasters that he and Hannah had nearly run completely amok practically over their heads, Joan would be sprawled on the floor in a scandalized coma.* "Good morning, Deacon," she said with as much poise as she could muster. Then to the general table, added, "I'm sorry I'm late, I was…" She paused, working on how to excuse her lateness without using words like "lust" and "insane."

"Oh, we know," Joan said, filling Hannah's pause. "Roth told us."

A quiver of dread skittered down her spine. What could he have said? She stared down at her plate, recently passed to her from Joan, who served scrambled eggs from a steaming bowl. "Oh?" she asked, then cringed. Why not let it go? Whatever he said couldn't have been what they really did. Even he wouldn't be that much of a jerk.

"Yes. He said it was his fault you were late."

She choked on a mouthful of eggs.

"Are you all right?" Joan asked.

Nodding, Hannah took a sip of water. "Yes—thank you," she wheezed, glancing at Roth. She wondered what he had said that he'd done that caused her to be late. *Not the truth!* she cried inwardly. *Please, anything but that!* He sipped his coffee, appearing not to be paying any attention to the conversation.

"Well, uh…" she began cautiously, unsure how to respond.

"I must admit, it's nice to have a talented male on the premises."

Hannah felt sick to her stomach. Exactly what kind of talent was Joan referring to? But how typical that Roth would make himself the star of their little epic, whatever it might be.

"A close call, but in the end, no great tragedy, so no real harm done."

That cryptic remark worried her. It sounded a little too near the truth for comfort, but she didn't dare comment.

"He saved his ring." Joan sighed deeply. "How fortunate that he had tools and could take apart the sink drain to retrieve it."

Hannah glanced at Roth. He seemed to sense it and turned to meet her gaze. Laying down his butter knife, he held up his left hand, exhibiting his college class ring. "Good as new," he said, his grin nothing more than a show of teeth. His eyes held a darkness she dared not attempt to read. "I told them my tinkering made you have to take a late bath."

She swallowed hard. His tinkering indeed! She couldn't find her voice, so she shrugged, broke eye contact and toyed with her food.

"Speaking of talented men," Joan said, "Deacon was kind enough to drop by to fix the toaster. It tended to fling toast at the ceiling. It works fine now, so naturally, I insisted he stay for breakfast."

"I was happy to help," Deacon said. Hannah made herself look up and focus on him. He smiled at her. She smiled, too, though she sensed her effort was a bit weak. She wasn't over the scare with the "Roth made you late" statement and had an urge to kick him under the table. Not to mention the "tinkering" remark.

"Hannah?" Deacon said, breaking into her reverie. He smiled when she looked over at him. "Joan offered to fix a picnic lunch for me and a guest, and I wondered if you'd like to join me?"

She stared, startled by the invitation. "Today?"

He nodded. "If it's convenient."

She glanced at Joan. The older woman grinned like an Olympic athlete who'd just won gold. "You didn't have any plans, did you, dear?"

"Well, I…" Hannah hesitated and wondered why.

"Fried chicken, potato salad, sliced tomatoes and cake," Joan said. Then to Mona and Roth. "Of course, we'll have the same menu—just here."

Hannah felt trapped, but considering the alternative—sitting so close to Roth at the noon meal—she decided a picnic with Deacon would be less stressful. "Well, sure, Deacon, if you don't have to work."

"He has a capable staff," Joan said quickly.

Deacon smiled the charming smile she was sure turned a lot of women to mush. She wished it affected her that way. "Thursdays are traditionally pretty crime-free," he kidded.

"I hadn't heard that," Roth said.

Hannah recognized his remark as sarcasm. "I'm sure the sheriff wasn't referring to national statistics."

"True. I meant in Delaware county," Deacon said.

"Ah." Roth nodded, as though vastly enlightened. This time Hannah couldn't help herself and whacked him on the ankle with the edge of her jogging shoe.

"Ouch," he said.

"Something wrong, Mr. Johnson?" Joan asked.

He cleared his throat, and to his credit didn't turn to glare at Hannah. "I, er, bit my tongue."

"What a shame." Hannah fought the urge to smirk. "I hate it when that happens. And doesn't it always seem like you bite the same place over and over? I certainly hope you *don't*—do it again." She trusted he could read her coded threat.

He glanced her way and smiled blandly. "Miss Hudson, your concern warms my heart."

"Think nothing of it. And I really mean *nothing*." She lifted her mug of coffee and held it toward him in a salute she was sure he would recognize for the mocking gesture it was.

"Well…" Roth planted the flats of his hands on the table and pushed up. "I have business in Grove, so if you all will excuse me?"

"I think we can muddle along," Hannah murmured, the mug at her lips.

Joan giggled. Hannah knew if her hostess heard, so did Roth. Fine. Excellent! What did she care? In a voice she knew would carry to Roth as he exited, she added, "I haven't been on a picnic in forever, Deacon. I'm delighted you invited me."

She experienced such a release of stress with Roth's departure, she came close to batting her lashes at the sheriff.

CHAPTER SIX

HANNAH'S picnic with Deacon ended abruptly, thanks to a jack-knifed tractor-trailer truck and its spilled load of honeybees, honeycomb and honey, causing chaos just north of Sailboat Bridge. When she entered the inn, two things hit her, the lingering smell of paint, and Joan Peterson.

Joan's collision was more an excited hug than an actual hit. "How was it?" She released Hannah's shoulders and grabbed her hands. "Did you have a good time?" The older woman's eyes sparkled with expectation. She had it in her mind that Hannah and Deacon were perfect for each other, and it would be hard to convince her that the chemistry just wasn't there. More than a little bit, Hannah wished it were. Life would be simpler.

She couldn't understand herself. Why, of all the people in the world, did she have to have this shocking, wayward attraction for Roth Jerric. She didn't even like the man.

With a determined smile, Hannah disengaged herself from Joan's grip. "The picnic was very nice. And the food was wonderful."

"Thank you, dear," Joan said. Hannah could almost read the question, *Did he kiss you?* in Joan's eyes. It was so obvious, Hannah felt embarrassed. "He, uh, had to go, though, an accident on the other side of Sailboat Bridge."

Joan's expression clouded. "Oh? How vexing for you both."

Hannah had a feeling it was more "vexing" for Joan than for either Hannah or Deacon. Deacon might be attracted to her, but not enough to burn away his lingering grief over the loss of his wife. Hannah had the feeling he was actually *trying* to be attracted to her. Maybe he thought it was time to move on, and Hannah had appeared on the horizon at the right moment. It was more a case of being well-timed than well-loved.

Fearing she might blurt out that—no, there had been no kissing or even great urges in that direction—she brushed away some grass clinging to her jeans, and changed the subject. "I think I'll take a bath. Afterward, I'll help you prepare supper."

"That's sweet of you," Joan said. "Then you can tell me all about it."

Hannah winced. It seemed the "No, he didn't kiss me" confession would be hanging over her head for a while.

"Oh," Joan said, as though the thought just struck, "I have some nice news about Mr. Johnson."

Hannah was momentarily confused, then realized she meant Roth Jerric. "Really?" She feigned nonchalance. Why did the mere mention of his name—even when it wasn't his name— make her heart race. "Did he check out?"

Joan giggled and shook her head. "No, no." She patted Hannah's arm. "We're not going to be upset with him anymore because he did the most adorable thing."

Hannah couldn't imagine what he could have done to completely turn Joan around from contentious to chummy. "What adorable thing did he do?"

"The sweet man went into town and paid the back taxes I owe. Isn't that wonderful? And I've harbored such harsh thoughts about him, too. I feel so ashamed."

Hannah frowned. She wasn't up on Tax Lien Certificates and Tax Deed Sales, but she had a feeling Roth's act was less adorable than scheming. "He told you what he did?"

"Yes," Joan said. "He said he wants to help me better my situation."

"Hmm." Hannah didn't dare comment yet, but she figured Roth was laying the groundwork to line his own pockets. After a certain amount of time he could use those tax certificates to steal Joan's home out from under her. She wanted badly to tell Joan about Roth's ulterior motives. No, she must wait until she could confront Roth, make sure his aim was as black-hearted as she believed.

"We mustn't think badly of him."

"Where is he?" Hannah asked. "I'd like to tell him how adorable *I* think he is for what he did."

"I believe he's in his room."

"Good." Hannah took Joan's hand and squeezed. "I'll be down in a while."

"No hurry, dear," Joan called as Hannah bounded up the stairs.

At Roth's door, Hannah hesitated. "Count to ten," she whispered. "Don't assume the worst. Simply ask the man what his intention was in paying her back taxes." She inhaled deeply and let it out. "If he responds with anything but 'I'm stealing her home' then go ahead and murder the lying SOB!"

With one more deep inhale and slow, calming exhale, she knocked.

"Yes?"

"May I come in?"

A pause, then, "Of course."

Once inside his room she realized what he must think. She felt uncomfortable, too aware of what went on behind those narrowed, calculating eyes. He thought she had changed her mind about having sex with him. What an ego he must have!

He lounged on his bed. His legs were stretched out and crossed at the ankles. Thank heaven, he was fully clothed in jeans and a beige knit shirt. He held his cell phone to his ear.

"That's it for now." He flipped the cell closed and laid it on the bedside table. Directing his full attention on Hannah, he smiled. "This is an unexpected pleasure."

She experienced a lurch in her chest and steeled herself against it. "It's not a social call."

One dark eyebrow quirked upward. "No?"

"No," she said. "It's business."

He tilted his head, querying, "A proposition?"

Innuendo dripped from his comment. Or did it? Why did she get so disoriented and confused around the man? She wrenched her gaze away from her absurd preoccupation with his face, focusing instead on his loafers. She crossed her arms, then uncrossed them. Why couldn't she find something to do with her hands? Antsy, she plunged them into her jeans pockets. "No, just a question," she said, her voice raspy. Against her will, her gaze slid to his face. Exasperated with his animal magnetism, she demanded straight out, "Why did you pay Joan's back taxes? And *don't* lie."

His expression grew inquiring. "Why would I lie?"

"Don't evade the question with a question, either."

He slid his legs off the bed, and stood. "Okay, yes, I paid them."

"Why?" she challenged.

His eyebrows dipped as though he were disappointed that she had to ask.

"So, I'm right," she charged. "You are trying to steal her home out from under her."

One broad shoulder rose and fell in a casual shrug. "She still has plenty of time to pay back what she owes, plus penalties. If she does, she keeps her home and I get an eight percent dividend. You could think of it as an investment."

"You won't mind if I don't," she said. "You know it's not likely she can come up with the taxes, let alone penalties."

"I don't know anything of the kind."

Hannah's exhale was guttural, very like a curse. "How can

you be so heartless? This is her home! You know how she feels about it."

He walked toward her, his features serious. "It was my home once. When I was a kid. Trust me, it's just a house. Besides, if she's going to lose her home to someone, don't you think it's better that it's me? At least I plan to provide for her, give her a modern, comfortable condo, paid for and worry free."

"And memories free, charm free, and happiness free," she threw back.

He kept coming. She backed up and hit the door with a painful thud. "Would you rather some stranger get the property, who would throw her out, leaving her with nothing and nowhere to go?"

"But—but the Blue Moon Inn is worth saving, just as it is with all its old-fashioned quaintness and appeal."

"Like the rusty pipes, peeling paint and sagging roof?"

"Yes. All those things, plus the tranquil woods, the breezy screened porch. Even the squeak in the porch swing. How can you not love the antique clawfoot tubs and solid pecan floors? If it was your home once, then you, of all people, should see there's so much about this inn that, once gone, can never be recovered."

"It's foolish to let emotions get in the way of intelligent thinking. Emotions have no place in business."

"Emotions are part of life," she shot back. "Even in business. For women, it is very much about how you are perceived in your job. And when your boss thinks of you as..." She balked at saying it aloud, so she decided to go on the offensive. "You should open up emotionally, find out what it's like to be a living, breathing human being once in a while. Try *feeling* just a little bit."

He laughed, the sound bitter. "Feel? Oh, I've felt plenty, and it's a mistake I choose not to make, again."

"Again?" she asked, her curiosity piqued. "Are you saying you've known the joys and the pain of being alive? I don't believe it!"

He stalked closer. "I don't care what you believe."

She knew what to do with her hands now. She held them out in a classic Stop signal. "Don't come any closer." She was furious, true, but she remembered all too vividly what had almost happened in this room earlier today, and she wasn't convinced Roth didn't have magical powers. If he got too near, she was afraid this time she might crumble completely.

He stopped, stared, as though physically struck. "I'm not going to attack you."

She knew that, but she didn't plan to explain her problem with his nearness. "You know what?" she demanded, her decision quick and final. "I'm going to offer my services to Joan. I'm a good financial manager, no matter that you think I'm mediocre!"

"Would you quit telling me what I think! Besides, when did I—"

"Don't interrupt." She was horrified she'd actually said the awful "M" word out loud. She wanted to get out of there, and fast. But beyond that, she had also blurted out a terrifically consequential inspiration. Rash or not, she suddenly could see it all as clear as day. *That* was the answer to her career dilemma. Why hadn't she thought of it before? This inn would be an altogether different work environment. A small town, someplace cozy, where she'd feel like family, suddenly seemed right.

Yes, absolutely! Managing the Blue Moon Inn was the answer. "If Joan will have me, I'm going to take over running this place. I'll turn the Blue Moon Inn around, make it profitable. You hide and watch." She was not mediocre and putting Joan's inn in the black would prove it, if anything would. "And don't worry, Mr. Jerric, I'll make sure you get your eight percent— and *nothing* more."

His lips twisted cynically. "She can't pay you a salary."

"I'll work for room and board until we're in the black."

His eyes sharp and assessing, he asked, "Why butt into something that's none of your business?"

"I'm making it my business. I plan to help Joan fight your buyout—for love."

"Love?" he repeated with icy sarcasm. "After only a few days you love this place so much you'd throw yourself, your savings, maybe even your career away on a lost cause?"

"Yes! For the love of keeping something small and quaint free of corporate blight, yes, I'd risk all that."

He shook his head. "You should fit in fine." His jaw muscles flexed, a clear indicator of his disapproval. "You're nuts, too."

"I'd rather be nuts than a greedy, arrogant ass."

He took a step toward her and she instinctively threw up a protective arm.

He stilled; a stricken look flashed across his face, as though her show of fear pained him. With a coarse growl, he encircled her waist with his hands and lifted her out of his way. "This has been fun," he ground out. "Drop by anytime."

A moment later the door slammed shut and she was alone.

As Hannah descended the stairs, fresh from her bath and ready to help with supper, a keening wail spilled from the kitchen. Frightened that Joan had hurt herself, she dashed down the rest of the stairs, skidded around the corner and careened along the hall to the kitchen door. "What happened?" she cried, breathless, scanning Joan for signs of spurting blood.

"It's Miss Mischief." Joan wadded a handkerchief in front of her mouth and sat down heavily at the kitchen table. "She's missing. She's old, arthritic and half blind. Somehow she slipped out of the house. I've looked everywhere and called and called, but she hasn't come to me." Her voice broke. "I'm afraid something horrible has happened to my baby girl."

Hannah felt deep empathy for Joan's anguish and sharp concern for the dog's welfare. "What can I do to help?"

Joan twisted the handkerchief between her fists. "I don't know what else to do but mount a search. She's probably gotten disoriented and lost. She's out there somewhere frightened, maybe injured."

"I'll go look for her right away," Hannah said. "Unless you need me to help make supper."

"I'd rather we all search. There are plenty of leftovers, fried chicken, potato salad. We can make do snacking on that. I simply can't rest until we find Missy Mis." She stifled a sob with the wadded kerchief. "She's hurt, I know she's hurt. Maybe dead. Or drowned. She can't swim well anymore. Oh, she's dead, I know she's dead."

"Please, don't dwell on the worst. I'm sure she's just wandered off and she's fine." Hannah hugged the older woman. "I'll get Mona."

"She's already searching." Joan pointed in the direction of the garden and church ruins. "Over that way." She pushed herself up awkwardly. "You and Ross take the woods to the east. I'll check the front, toward the road."

"Oh, I, uh…" Hannah didn't have any intention of searching with Roth Jerric. But in view of Joan's distress, she decided not to burden the woman with her problems. Instead she nodded "I'll alert Roth." There were lots of woods to go around. They could both search and never have to cross paths. "Where is he?"

"He was swimming earlier." She placed a quivery hand on her forehead. "I believe he went upstairs to dress for dinner."

"Okay. Don't worry. We'll find Missy Mis and she'll be fine. Mark my words." Hannah hurried from the kitchen and bounded back upstairs. At Roth's door, she struggled to maintain her composure. The last thing she wanted to do was knock on his door again. *Come now, Hannah,* she admonished inwardly. *You're not here to feed his bloated ego or even to remind him what an arrogant jerk he is. This is for Joan. Stop worrying about yourself and get on with it.* Her pep talk finished, she rapped smartly on the door. "Roth, I need to speak with you—immediately."

OFFICIAL OPINION POLL

ANSWER 3 QUESTIONS AND WE'LL SEND YOU
2 FREE BOOKS AND A FREE GIFT!

0074823 IIII▮II▮I▮III III▮▮IIII II▮IIIII   FREE GIFT CLAIM # **3953**

YOUR OPINION COUNTS!

Please check TRUE or FALSE below to express your opinion about the following statements:

Q1 Do you believe in "true love"?

"TRUE LOVE HAPPENS ONLY ONCE IN A LIFETIME." ○ TRUE ○ FALSE

Q2 Do you think marriage has any value in today's world?

"YOU CAN BE TOTALLY COMMITTED TO SOMEONE WITHOUT BEING MARRIED." ○ TRUE ○ FALSE

Q3 What kind of books do you enjoy?

"A GREAT NOVEL MUST HAVE A HAPPY ENDING." ○ TRUE ○ FALSE

YES, I have scratched the area below.

Please send me the 2 **FREE BOOKS** and **FREE GIFT** for which I qualify. I understand I am under no obligation to purchase any books, as explained on the back of this card.

386 HDL EFVV   186 HDL EFZV

FIRST NAME   LAST NAME

ADDRESS

APT.#   CITY

STATE/PROV.   ZIP/POSTAL CODE

www.eHarlequin.com

DETACH AND MAIL CARD TODAY!

(HTF-R-06/06)

The Harlequin Reader Service® — Here's how it works:

Accepting your 2 free books and mystery gift places you under no obligation to buy anything. You may keep the books and gift and return the shipping statement marked "cancel." If you do not cancel, about a month later we'll send you 6 additional books and bill you just $3.57 each in the U.S., or $4.05 each in Canada, plus 25¢ shipping & handling per book and applicable taxes if any.* That's the complete price and – compared to cover prices of $4.25 each in the U.S., and $4.99 each in Canada – it's quite a bargain! You may cancel at any time, but if you choose to continue, every month we'll send you 6 more books which you may either purchase at the discount price or return to us and cancel your subscription.

*Terms and prices subject to change without notice. Sales tax applicable in N.Y. Canadian residents will be charged applicable provincial taxes and GST.

If offer card is missing write to: The Harlequin Reader Service, 3010 Walden Ave., P.O. Box 1867, Buffalo, NY 14240-1867

She heard no response and toyed with the idea of getting away before she did. No, that would be cowardly. As she lifted her fist to knock again, the door swung wide.

Roth stood there, wrapped in a towel, deliciously male, his torso glinting with moisture, his wet hair mussed charmingly. Too charmingly. He looked "movie-coiffed-mussed," like leading men look in films, not honest-to-goodness men who just stepped from the shower. Had he really just bathed, or had he spent an hour standing before his mirror artfully mussing his hair and spritzing himself with water to give that impression—in case some vulnerable female came to his door?

What an absurd thought! She mentally shook herself. She could detect the scent of soap. He smelled wonderful—just like this morning when—

"Sorry for the delay," he said, interrupting her backsliding thoughts. "I grabbed a towel." He tilted his head in inquiry, his expression sardonic. "I trust you don't mind."

His needling was working. She resented him for his ability to unsettle her, annoy her and arouse her at the same time. "Uh, I, Joan…" She stuttered to a halt. Good grief. She'd lost her train of thought. Why was she here?

Sparking mockery invaded his stare. "No, you Hannah. Me, Roth," he said. "Now that we have that cleared up, is there anything else?"

The reason she knocked on his door came screaming back. "Yes, there is. Joan's dog is missing. The poor woman is terribly upset. We're all going to fan out and search. You and I are assigned the woods to the east." She felt restless faced with all that beautifully male flesh. She adding impatiently, "It wasn't my idea to search with you, and I don't plan on it. We can comb the woods—separately."

He pursed his lips, obviously more introspective than overcome by the news. "There's no reason for hysteria," he said. "That dog has lived here all its life. It's not going to get lost."

She hadn't expected such a cold-blooded reaction. Planting her fists on her hips, she said, "Maybe you didn't understand. The dog is already lost. Are you saying you won't help hunt for her?"

"I'm saying it's pure emotionalism and a waste of time and energy." He lifted his forearm above his head and leaned it on the doorjamb, curling his fingers around it. "Country dogs are accustomed to open spaces. They roam their domain. She's happy. Trust me. She'll be back when she's ready."

Hannah couldn't believe her ears. "Missy Mis is old, arthritic, can hardly see. She goes outside on a leash. Have you ever seen that dog spend five minutes away from Joan's side? How can you suggest that old mutt is out there happily exploring. That's absurd."

As she spoke she noticed a distinct hardening of his eyes. Clearly he had no intention of helping. Frustrated, she blurted, "You really are a heartless jerk. I can't believe I almost let you—" Unnerved that she'd said even that much to remind them both of this morning's indiscretion—as if she needed any reminder—she spun away, embarrassed. She needed to get away from the sight and scent of this man. It was making her crazy.

Besides, poor Missy Mis was lost and standing here beating her head against this bullheaded, arrogant brick wall of a man was a waste of good daylight. She hurried toward the stairs and began running down them two at a time. "I'll search the woods by myself," she shouted. "You know where *you* can go!"

Gloom shrouded the breakfast table like an overcast sky. All by herself, Hannah fried eggs and bacon and cooked Mona's oatmeal. Joan was too exhausted and distraught to do anything but weep and whisper Missy Mis's name in despairing moans. Her eyes swollen and red-rimmed, she slumped at the table, but didn't touch her food. Mona stirred her cereal, eyes downcast.

Deacon joined in the search early that morning, but no sign had been found of the dog. Hannah tried to eat, but couldn't force food past the lump in her throat.

Roth had not appeared for breakfast, which was just as well. Hannah's fury at him for his lack of support raged at a murderous level. Considering Joan's desolation, she might be forced to strangle him, even with the sheriff as a witness.

She looked at Deacon, who watched her. They exchanged unhappy nods. "After breakfast, I'll drop by the Wilson place," he said, clearly trying to appear upbeat. "Missy Mis could have wandered over there. They're new enough to the lake that they wouldn't know whose dog she is."

"Doesn't her collar have the inn's phone number?" Hannah asked, then bit her tongue. She could see in Deacon's expression explicit disappointment of her reminder.

"She could have lost her collar," he said, trying to prevent another burst of sobbing from their hostess.

"Oh—right. That's true." Hannah nodded vehemently. "That happens all the time." She had no idea if it did or not, but she had to redeem herself for making things worse.

"It was an old collar," Joan murmured hopefully, sniffling into her handkerchief. "Do go there, Deke." Longing shimmered in her bloodshot eyes.

A bang echoed from the kitchen entrance, then a miraculous sound. A bark. And a second. The familiar *tippy-tap* of Missy Mis's paws bolting down the hallway was a sound right out of heaven. For an instant the would-be diners surrounding the table searched each other's faces, the unspoken question, *"Could it be?"*

An instant later, in one swift upsurge, everybody bailed from the table to see. Though Deacon and Hannah were faster, they allowed Joan to be the first person into the hall. Her eyes went wide and she cried out, *"Missy Mis! My love, my baby!"* Slowly and awkwardly going down on her knees, she held out her arms. The aged, gray dog ran into her embrace, licking her face and whimpering joyfully.

Hannah could tell Missy Mis had spent a rough night by her muddy coat and the burrs caught in her fur. Otherwise, she looked healthy enough.

Another sound came from the direction of the kitchen. Hannah glanced up in time to see Roth in the doorway. He wore jeans and a soft, ribbed cotton V-neck shirt, the same blue as his eyes. He looked a little worse for wear, his jeans and hiking boots caked with mud, burrs stuck in the denim, on the shirt. Even a few clung to his hair. His expression was set, his jaw hard. His eyes sparked with some indefinable emotion. A splash of mud dirtied his cheek, but did nothing to mar his masculine charisma. On the contrary, the blemish made him seem more accessible, human and, if possible, even more desirable.

Obviously Roth had found Missy Mis. She couldn't quite absorb it, so she simply stared, frowning her confusion. "What did you do?" she asked over the hubbub of relieved exclamations.

His eyes took on a burning, faraway look. His cheek muscles bunched with what Hannah felt was self-conscious reluctance to explain himself. He shook his head and made for the stairs, angling deftly around the gathered crowd. Hannah grasped his hand. "You changed your mind?" she asked.

He glanced at her, but quickly broke eye contact. "I had a dog once," he said, matter-of-factly, but she didn't believe he felt matter-of-fact. "He got lost. I was five, too young to be allowed to go search for him. I never saw him again." He removed his hand from her grip. "I remembered how I felt."

He walked away, down the hall and around the corner. Conflicted, Hannah watched him go. Here was a man, heartlessly doing his best to steal Joan's home, yet he'd spent a good part of the night searching for her decrepit old dog.

The shimmer of pain in his eyes over the memory of a long-lost pet affected her strongly. In the time it took for him to say,

"I remembered how I felt," her dislike and animosity for him dissolved; in its place rushed an upsurge of yearning. She battled a need to run to him and kiss him hard—again and again. Such a profound, all-consuming reaction to his one, small selfless act frightened her.

CHAPTER SEVEN

THE past twenty-four hours hadn't been Roth's most rational, from the wildly illogical near seduction of Hannah, to the dog rescue. Both unlike him; he'd acted like somebody he didn't even know.

He stepped into the shower to wash away all traces of the night's grubby extrication. Sometime around 2:00 a.m., he remembered a narrow cavern where Miss Mischief might have fallen. The grotto was nearly invisible unless you knew about it, and even harder to escape from, if you happened to be a small, four-legged creature with an arthritic hip. As a kid, he found the narrow rift in the rocky terrain the hard way, by tumbling in. Once discovered, it became a pirate's lair, a space ship or an outlaw hideout. In other words, a paradise for a young boy's imagination.

Due to the topography, he knew the dog's barks would be almost inaudible. A searcher could pass within ten feet and never know it was there. So, in honor of a long lost pet, he spent much of the night in an effort to locate and rescue Joan's mutt. The wooded environs had changed over the years, with old tree landmarks gone, downed by age or storms, replaced by newer growth. Then there was the problem that it was the middle of the night. The woods were black and choked with underbrush.

A dead oak lay across the earthen cavity, so Roth crisscrossed the area for hours before relocating the site. When he finally did and clambered inside, sure enough, the dog was there, huddled at the bottom of the crevice, dirty, frightened and hungry.

The satisfaction he felt locating that mongrel, experiencing her shivery joy as he clutched her to his chest climbing out, somehow made up for a hell of a lot. Like his guilt for not going to search when Hannah asked. He supposed he was still stinging about how she had left him that morning, and then her flirty acceptance of the sheriff's invitation to go picnicking. He'd been upset and hurt, and angry that he'd been upset and hurt. So when Hannah came to his door asking for help, he had lashed out, taking his frustration out on her and a helpless dog.

He yawned, so sleep deprived he could hardly stand up. He shook off his aching fatigue and soaped his chest, enjoying the stream of warm water easing the exhaustion from his bones. He didn't even mind the groan and shudder of the antiquated pipes. He had come back to his childhood home to regain an exuberance he'd lost in the years since starting his oil business. He had found a rebirth of that exuberance in his plans for Joan's property. Then, like some kind of avenging angel, Hannah Hudson swooped in, wielding her "Oh-no-you-don't" sword of contention and divisionism.

He found her interference as pesky as hell. That should have been enough to make him keep his distance. Yet, seeing her on the balcony yesterday morning drove him a little crazy. That blasted breeze pressed the fabric of her light, cotton robe against curvy bits of femininity, provoking and testing him, lifting the short hem to reveal appealing glimpses of trim, pale thighs.

It was at that moment she had turned and noticed him, going still, her lips opening ever so slightly. Those unusual, striking eyes went wide with surprise and disquiet, charming and arousing him against his will. The impact of all those things, piled one on another, was so powerful he felt it like a brick in the chest.

He felt something else, too. Though less tangible its effect was every bit as compelling. He could only describe it as a silken thread binding them together. Though delicate, that tiny, golden string contained the strength of steel—woven from tension and temptation, from secret glances and impetuous touches. The bond was there, connecting them, pulling them inevitably toward one another, the outcome as inescapable as the march of time. Or so he'd thought until Hannah had put an abrupt, painful stop to it.

He wasn't proud of what he'd almost done, yet neither was he sorry. If he were honest with himself, he was damn confused. The fact that she made it her business to defeat his purchase of the inn aggravated him mightily. However, for some bizarre reason her meddling didn't aggravate him enough to keep her from becoming a target for conquest.

He winced. Why? That's what yesterday morning's connection was meant to be, wasn't it? A conquest. The next in a long line of sexual trophies. He soaped his hair, then rinsed under the rush of water. Weary to the depths of his soul, he lifted his face, savoring the pelting current. He wasn't usually conflicted about one-time hookups. Ordinarily when they were over, he thought nothing more about them. Even on those rare occasions, like yesterday, when for whatever reason the sex didn't happen, he never thought about the woman again. He never felt guilty, good, bad, haunted or—anything. That was the way he chose to deal with his relationships with women. They were passing dalliances. They meant nothing, so he felt nothing. But this woman—this bothersome, exasperating woman—why couldn't he get her out of his head?

All in, he turned off the water to an accompanying shudder from the handles. Pushing his hands through his hair, he sloughed off excess moisture. "I'm just tired." He muttered the lie aloud, hoping hearing it would make it reality. In truth, the moment Hannah left his bed, a part of him began to ache, an ache he neither understood nor had any hope of healing. Nevertheless, he intended to lie to himself as long as it took to turn the damn fiction into fact. "All I need is sleep."

He drew the shower curtain aside and grew stock-still. To his amazement Hannah stood before the bathtub, her breathtaking eyes wide, her expression solemn, almost sad.

"What the hell?" he said, awe in his tone.

She didn't immediately respond. After a heartbeat, she untied the sash of her robe and shrugged it off her shoulders. Without a sound it fell in a heap at her feet. Naked, she faced him, proudly, though he could detect ambivalence and fragility in her eyes.

"I can't think of a single reason why I'm here," she whispered.

If she were only a little less beautiful, a little less tempting, he might have been able to resist as logic and reason told him he should. But the sight of her standing there, offering herself so sweetly, yet solemnly, made him moral mush, unable to turn her away.

He hungered to know the full depth and breadth of the beauty they came so close to sharing not so long ago. A beauty, until this moment, he believed he would never taste.

He wasn't a weak man, but somehow, right now, something in Hannah's eyes made him so. Casting aside wisdom, he took her hand. "Maybe, together…" he murmured, drawing her into the tub, "we can think of a reason."

Hannah knew her spontaneity could be a flaw, but to do something so utterly senseless and destructive as to walk naked into that tub with Roth Jerric, knowing full well they would have sex—all because he rescued Joan's dog—well, it had to be the most disastrous mistake of her life!

"Idiot! Idiot! Idiot!" She pounded her pillow. Not only was

it stupidity with a capital STUPID, but it was now keeping her awake with—of all things—a steamy, seething need to be held in *his* arms again, of all people on earth. She hated herself for being so frail of both character and conviction.

Restless and angry, she jumped out of bed eager to move, to work off her restless energy. She needed to funnel it into a less dangerous exercise. In the dark, she grabbed the shorts and top she wore that day and, barefoot, hurried down the stairs and out the kitchen door, heading toward the lake. She recalled seeing a rowboat that had been hauled up onto a muddy out-cropping of land. At Jerric Oil she spent her lunch hour in the company gym, either spinning or on the rowing machine. Since there weren't any bikes around, she decided a little cruise around the cove would be just the ticket to tire her out enough to fall into dreamless sleep.

She hauled the old boat into the water and slipped in. As the boat bobbed away from shore, she settled the oars in the oar-locks, took a deep breath and began the job of forgetting about Roth and his lovemaking. Even in recollection she could feel the intimacy of his kisses, the delicious tickle when his lips left hers to nibble at her earlobe. The tender massage of his hands sending currents of desire through her. The exquisite caress of his body...

She closed her eyes, trying to make herself think of nothing at all. As she rowed, she gritted out, "I will not think about this morning in the shower." Naturally the very mention of the shower brought it all rushing back in a vivid wave of sensations, sounds and scents. How he took his time to explore, to arouse, to give her pleasure. So much pleasure. So much *guilty* pleasure. She heard a high-pitched cry and cringed with the realization that it had come from her own throat.

Ashamed of herself, she rowed with the zeal of the doomed in a futile bid to escape the inevitable. In her case, the "inevitable" was the endless regret of having learned that there existed such sensuous delights, such climactic satisfaction, between a man and woman.

"Why must I be forever cursed to have experienced such an apocalyptic truth from someone I should relentlessly denounce and most *certainly* deny!"

Hanging her head, she rowed with all her pent-up self-recriminations. Somewhere, somehow, in Roth Jerric's blue eyes she lost her moral compass and was adrift in a rough sea of remorse and confusion. The man didn't even think much of her, yet she dropped her robe and stepped into the tub, practically begging him to use her. Would this lapse be future fodder for testosterone-drenched locker room gossip?

Somewhere in Hannah's agonizing a tiny fact intruded. Her feet were wet. Not wet from wading into shallow water with the rowboat, but wet, as in "under water." Which shouldn't be, since her feet were inside the boat. Returned rudely to reality by this irony, she looked down at her lower extremities. Water lapped above her ankles. She frowned, able to come to only one conclusion. The boat had sprung a leak.

Hannah didn't swim well. She faced a bitter truth: the rowing machine at the office gym never presented this particular complication or prepared her for it. She never imagined the boat might not be fully functional. As water washed over her calves, she experienced a niggling touch of panic. The boat was now so awash in lake water it was too sluggish to steer, even pulling on the oars with all her strength. And worse, the bow of her craft faced away from shore.

She struggled to turn it, though she had a scary feeling even if she managed to aim toward shore, the sievelike hulk would be long submerged before she got halfway back.

Broadside to land, the bow dipped below the lake's surface. Water swept aboard, tipped the vessel sideways, tossing Hannah into the drink. In a desperate bid for survival she grabbed the stern, which by some miracle remained above water. Maybe it was held aloft by trapped air, maybe by Hannah's prayers. Whatever the reason, she had a reprieve from the Grim Reaper—at least for the moment.

She got a nose full of water, coughed and sputtered until her throat and chest hurt. Finally able to breathe again she became aware of how much her arms ached from gripping the splintery hull.

Though water lapped around her ears, she thought she heard her name being shouted. Was an angel calling her over to the other side? Not sure whether she was hallucinating or heading into the light, she shifted toward the sound. It seemed to come from the direction of shore, rather than from above.

"Hannah, hang on."

That voice sounded more earthly than ethereal, and awfully familiar. She caught the sparkle of splashing water in the moonlight. Someone swam toward her, and in the moonlight it wasn't hard to determine who. How did Roth know where she was, or that her boat was sinking? Besides everything else, was the man psychic? Or had her prayers been less silent than she thought? Had she shrieked them to high heaven?

In light of this new probability, her panic disappeared, replaced by such a thick blanket of self-accusation she could hardly stand being Hannah Hudson. *How could you let yourself go to pieces,* she admonished inwardly. *You can swim! Not well, but you can swim. Are you going to let him see you as deficient again? Are you going to let him think you're not only mediocre but a crybaby?*

She wished she had the power to zap him away with the blink of her eyes, whisking him back to his bed, asleep and oblivious. But she wasn't a TV witch. She had to deal with him in the here and now, preferably as a capable adult. "What are you doing?" she yelled, hoping she could bluff her way out of this mess.

He didn't respond, just kept surging forward with long, powerful strokes. The way he swam, he'd be there in another ten seconds.

"Roth!" she shouted. "Go back to bed. I'm fine."

He took another couple of strokes before he stopped his approach and began to tread water. "What?" he shouted.

"Go to bed." She released the boat with one arm and waved broadly in the direction of shore. "I'm okay."

"Then why were you yelling 'help me' at the top of your lungs?"

That might be tough to answer believably so she decided on the truth. "I panicked, so sue me. You can go. I'm fine."

"Yeah?" he asked. "Why are you clinging to a sinking boat?"

She hesitated, at a loss. "I—I was catching my breath."

"I hope you've caught it," he said, "Because the boat's about to go."

On cue the stern slipped below the surface with a gurgle. She swallowed spasmodically, feeling very alone. But shame for her weakness for Roth Jerric mixed with her cumbersome pride wouldn't allow her to let him near her, even to save her life.

Kicking madly to keep her head above water, she said, "I'm a competent adult. I can swim to shore without your—your interference." She took a deep breath and aimed for land. "Just—just go back to bed."

He remained where he was, treading water, about two car lengths away. She checked the distance to shore. Maybe three tennis courts strung end to end. She could swim that far, couldn't she? Just because she never had before, didn't mean she couldn't tonight. Surely her determination and innate survival instinct would kick in enough to make up for any shortcomings in ability.

"Hannah," he said, sounding aggravated. "Part of being competent is knowing when to ask for help."

"Oh? Well part of *not* being annoying is *not* giving people advice they don't want," she shouted, grateful she didn't swallow a mouthful of water in the process. She'd never progressed beyond the dog paddle, so she paddled furiously. Why did she have such a tendency to sink? Were her hips so disproportionately bulky her upper body strength wasn't up to hefting their weight? She could feel her lower half angling down. With cupped hands and thrashing legs she pulverized the water, chugging along with all her might, straining to keep her head above the surface.

She flailed, sank, struggled up coughing and wheezing, paddled some more, went under, came up snorting and spitting, making precious little progress.

Suddenly she found herself beside Roth. Had she swum that far or had he sneaked up on her? Whichever, it was time for her to face facts. She wasn't going to make it by herself and she would not *really* rather drown than ask for help. She was prideful but not a fool. She grasped his shoulder, panting. "Okay—I—need…" She broke off, hacking out a mouthful of water.

"Happy to." He began to swim toward shore in a smooth breaststroke. "Hold on with both hands."

She didn't have much fight left, and no voice at all, so she took him up on his offer. All too soon her descending lower half ran into his legs. "I'm sorry. I tend to sink."

"Wrap your legs around my waist."

She feared herself around him and hesitated. "Is that necessary?"

He treaded water, keeping them both afloat. His expression serious, he said, "Would you rather I drag you back to shore by your hair?"

She raised her chin defiantly, which lost much of its punch, since her chin was under water. "No need to go all Neanderthal."

"It's a rescue hold," he said. "Or I could slip under you and use the hold where I grab you across the chest."

She ran a hand through her hair to clear dripping tendrils

from her eyes. The hair hold would be safest—sensually speaking. She stalled, torn by conflicting urges.

"Make up your mind," he said. "I'd like to get some sleep tonight."

"Okay, okay." Hurriedly, she grasped his shoulders. "Start swimming. I'll do the, uh, waist thing."

"Great." His tone spoke volumes. He might as well have said, *You're driving me crazy, and not in a good way.*

He began the breaststroke again. When her bottom half did its usual dive, she encircled his waist with her legs. A few strokes later she began to have trouble holding on to his shoulders with her hands. The water made him slippery. She hurriedly hugged his neck, which brought her face up next to his ear. "I was having trouble holding on. Is this okay, or am I in the way?" she asked, not wanting to interfere with his swimming.

"I like your arms around me," he said.

She was so undone by his frankness and so frightened by her own growing desire, she let go and immediately began to flounder. She went under. A second later, she felt herself being pulled up. Her head broke the surface and she sucked in a gulp of blessed air.

"Why I keep bringing you to the surface I'll never know," he said. "I've never met a woman so fickle. You go from hot to cold faster than a gas range. Have you ever managed to have an actual relationship?"

She coughed to clear her throat. "*Focus!* I'm drowning here."

He growled out a curse. "Grab on." He pulled her close so she could encircle his neck with her arms. "I'll keep my thoughts to myself and just taxi you to dry land."

"Thanks," she said, unable to keep a grudging edge from her voice. She wrapped her legs around his waist again, trying not to think about how delicious he felt.

They glided toward shore and she marveled at him, swimming with such power and finesse. He certainly wasn't a mediocre swimmer. Was he mediocre at anything? If she could only find the man's Achilles' heel, how she would rejoice.

Hannah, she scolded mutely, *it's sad to be such a failure that you could even think about rejoicing to find Roth's Achilles' heel, especially while he's saving your life.*

She hugged him. Unwillingly she experienced a surge of sweet gratification in the tantalizing male stretch and bunch of muscle. *Why, oh why,* she cried internally, *has fate decreed that Roth not only continually witness my defeats, but that he must also inspire and collaborate in the most scandalous of them?*

CHAPTER EIGHT

THEY reached the shallows. Roth stood and began to walk. When the water was hardly more than waist high, he said, "Do you intend for me to carry you all the way back to your room?"

Hannah had been so lost in emotional turmoil his remark didn't make sense at first. "Hmm?" she asked.

"You probably won't drown now, unless you breathe through your knees."

She heard sloshing as he moved into ever shallower water. Lord, she still clung to him. "Oh—sorry." She let go and slid into the water. By the time she found her footing he was several paces ahead. Moonlight paid homage to his broad shoulders, strong back, firm tush and muscular thighs. Gritting her teeth, she forced herself to look away. Her gaze lifted to the inn and she noticed her window was dark while his blazed with light.

"I didn't wake you, then," she thought out loud.

"What?" He shifted to peer at her, showing off a tempting chunk of chest muscle.

She wished she hadn't engaged him in conversation. It would have been better to let him walk away—end of rescue, end of story. She shrugged. "Never mind. I was thinking aloud."

He frowned, turned away and sloshed to shore. On dry land, he surprised her by dropping to the grass to lie on his back. He laced his fingers behind his head and stared up at the sky. She watched him, his chest expanding with each intake of breath. He seemed winded. She supposed she shouldn't be surprised, with Utterly Sinkable Hannah Hudson lashed to him like a sack of cement.

She fought an urge to lie down beside him, and continued her march toward the inn. His hand whipped out to encompass her ankle, startling her so badly she nearly stumbled. His hold was painless but firm. "Going so soon?" he asked.

"I—I thought I would." It's not what she thought at all, but it was the safe thing to do. With no choice but to come to a stop, she looked down at him.

One hand remained beneath his head as he met her gaze; his lips curved in a half smile. "Stay. Keep me company."

She saw desire flicker in his eyes and knew exactly what he thought was going to happen next. And why shouldn't he? She hadn't played very hard to get. But mistakes were to be learned from. Especially extraordinarily stupid ones. She shook her head. "I don't think it's a good idea."

He angled his head, eyes narrowing as though he were skeptical and deciding how much coaxing she needed in order to change her mind. Fearing it wouldn't take much, she tugged on his hold. "Let me go, please."

He ignored her, his fingers, warm and snug, claimed her ankle. His thumb began to brush along the sensitive inner depression beneath the ankle bone, a whispery coercion she could not endure long without crumbling. Growing panicked, she cried, "I said no."

He loosened his hold, though his thumb continued to stroke, meltingly persuasive. A few more feathery caresses and she would be lost. "No means no," she said. "Let me go."

"I'm not holding you." He proved his statement by spreading his fingers, though his thumb continued its velvety massage. That light, delicious flesh to flesh contact held her with the same ferocity as an iron band. Why wasn't she running for her life?

Once he made his point, he allowed his hands to curl lightly around her ankle again. Now they both knew nothing held her there but her own longing.

"You ought to learn to swim," he said casually. "I'll teach you."

Her thoughts had taken a sharp turn elsewhere. Being brought back so abruptly from the brink of surrender to her recent near-drowning, she resisted even the idea of doing anything with him. He was too stimulating to be around. "I can swim."

"Not well enough that anybody can tell." He spoke softly and she felt no bite in his rebuke. His thumb began to circle her ankle bone seductively, making thinking difficult. "Let me," he whispered.

Somehow his soft "let me" didn't sound like he still referred to swimming lessons. It felt more like a hypnotist's instruction. She was definitely caught in his spell. Her resistance swiftly ebbing, she knew it was either give in to the lessons or to something much more damaging to her self-respect.

He was right. She should learn to swim. She could have died out there. "Yes—yes—okay..." Her acquiescence came out breathy, strange to her ears. She was in trouble. His touch, the gentle rubbing along her ankle, crippled her defenses. The last of her resistance fading, she slipped from his touch. "I need..." Her voice caught and she sucked in a restorative breath.

"What?" he asked, his tone arresting. "What do you need?"

Lord, he expected her to say, *You! I need you! Take me! Do with me as you please. I'm lost without your kisses. Your touch makes my head spin, my body quiver. Make love to me and I soar to heaven.*

She came tragically close to saying exactly that. But she shored up her resolve. What kind of a woman would she be if she allowed a man to use her when she knew he thought of her as inferior? She reminded herself that she had grave differences with Roth Jerric, not only because of his low opinion of her abilities, but over the fate of the Blue Moon Inn.

*And don't forget your vow not to let a dominant male blunt
your good sense again. If ever there was a dominant male in this
world, Roth is that man.* "Swimming lessons," she said, a determined edge to her words. "I realize I *need* swimming lessons."

He drew up on an elbow and scanned her slowly from head
to foot. One eyebrow arched meaningfully. The drama of his
display made it plain he believed she hungered for something
much more gratifying than swimming lessons.

So what if he was right. She was weak for him and they both
knew it. She craved the textures, the juices, the flavors of his
body, ached for the heady sweetness of his loving. She wanted
nothing more than to know again the heat of him driving deep,
hard and hot inside her. Even the bawdy verbal tokens he whispered as he nipped at her willing flesh filled her with joy. All
these things she desperately hungered for, but resisted accepting with all her strength.

Her body rigid, her fists clenched, she bitterly admitted this
terrible reality—to herself. A growl of longing clawing at her
throat, she pledged upon pain of death, that Roth would never
hear any of this from her lips. She glared down at him. "The
self-satisfied arrogance of some men!" She spun away. "On second thought, I'd rather drown."

"Tomorrow. First lesson. Let's say ten," he called.

She slogged away, so overwrought she could hardly sputter
out a response. After a few more steps, she realized how foolish it was to allow her pride get the better of her. She had almost
drowned tonight. She did need to learn to swim. She halted, but
refused to face him. "I guess, I should," she said at last.

Panic began to niggle at her. Would she have the willpower
to resist him tomorrow? After all, they would be very close,
touching, and wearing extremely skimpy clothes. Worried and
eager to put emotional distance between them, she pivoted
back and pointed a finger in his direction. "One false move, and
you're a dead man."

His hawkish features were cruelly striking in the moonlight, even with the shadow of an ironic smile hovering at the corners of his lips. "You're welcome," he called back. "And it will be my pleasure."

Looking at him, all glisteny in soaked, clingy shorts, was dangerous. She whirled around and hurried off, muttering, "Not if I can help it."

One thing Roth learned about Hannah these past few days was the fact that, at times, she saw her own spontaneity as a flaw. They couldn't agree more on that. All too often her impulsiveness made him furious. But then, had she been more circumspect, she would never have stepped into that shower with him, and that would have been a crime. He couldn't recall a more awesome experience in his life.

Awesome? He hurried to correct himself. He didn't indulge in awesome experiences. Awesome was a word fraught with emotionalism. His life was logical, controlled, calculated. He turned off the shower, then stilled, a hard knot of ambivalence forming in his gut. "Damn me to Hades, it was awesome." Hannah's sexual spontaneity made him a better lover, more open—even vulnerable. The knot in his gut twisted and he groaned with the pain.

Long ago he buried his vulnerable side with the breakup of his marriage, never expecting or wanting to resuscitate it. But somehow, making love to Hannah, he felt unaccountably safe, allowed himself to be more relaxed, freer.

Another irony nagged at him. Her compassionate nature pulled him the way the moon pulled at the tide. Hannah cared for Joan, a woman she had only recently met. Through this brief acquaintanceship, she'd also made the rash, futile decision to attach herself and her occupational destiny to Joan's failing enterprise.

The headlong irrationality of her decision annoyed him, yet

the display of such compassion, with no evident selfish agenda, fascinated and drew him, too. Maybe there was something in the drinking water here that made people go slightly nuts, because lately he had become patently at odds with himself.

Giving his emotions free rein waylaid him once. He had been so hellishly wrong about Janice, so completely ambushed by her true, bloodless nature, he didn't trust himself to open up to anyone. Allowing himself to be vulnerable with Hannah was off the charts nuts. In his dealings, both personal and business, he'd come to rely on logic and reason, not histrionics and melodrama. In the case of women, sexual desire ruled the day. He was a polished lover and he'd never had any complaints, but in all honesty, the act, for him, had become mechanical and emotionally flat.

But with Hannah…

He bit off a curse, grabbed a towel and dried off. "I do not need this right now," he grumbled. "It's a new day. I'm fresher, my intellect fully in control." He hadn't come to his old family home to open up old wounds or fall into an impetuous affair. Janice had been his last emotional mistake. "Sex with Hannah only seemed better because it's been too long between women," he told himself. "Sometimes being a workaholic takes its toll in unexpected ways. That's all this is."

He tossed the towel in the hamper and went into his room. Grabbing his clothes from the dresser he tried to put his mind on other things. "But she's got spunk," he murmured, discovering thinking of other things might not be as easy as willing it. Hannah was no coward. He liked that about her, though her decisions weren't always well thought-out, unlike Roth, forever calculating the pros and cons of each situation.

That held especially true when it came to intimate relationships. He knew the folly of rushing blindly into a relationship. His heart, he vowed, would never again do his thinking.

He pulled on jeans, slipped on a soft, beige linen shirt,

stepped into suede dock shoes and headed downstairs for break-fast. As he entered the dining room he noticed the local sheriff relaxing at the head of the table. By now, even a house plant could understand what was going on. Joan Peterson was manipulating a romance between Hannah and Deacon.

Not that it bothered him.

With a smile that felt strained, he acknowledged the other male. "Your workday must begin early, Sheriff," he said. "Is the crime rate in this area particularly bad these days?" The fragrance of Hannah's shampoo lay pleasantly on the air. He inhaled more deeply than necessary as he gave Mona and Joan a friendly nod.

Deacon laughed. "Things are pretty quiet at the moment."

"I'm relieved." Roth took his seat, working to maintain his pleasant facade.

"Good morning, Ross." Joan picked up the sorghum pitcher and held it in his direction. "We were beginning to think you'd decided to sleep in."

Roth attempted to appear nonchalant. He'd slept damn badly last night. That midnight swim, with Hannah's body well, to put it mildly, her breasts burning into his back and those long, silky legs wrapped around him, had been more stimulating than sleep-inducing. "Sorry."

"No worries. I planned to keep a plate warm for you," Joan went on. "After all, if one can't sleep late on one's vacation, then when can one?"

He wasn't in the mood for banal chitchat, but tried not to let his surliness show. "One wouldn't know," he said, pouring the syrup over his pancakes. He held the small sorghum pitcher toward Hannah. Their hands grazed and their gazes met. He felt a zing of excitement and a stab of aggravation at the same instant, which didn't improve his mood. Her frown could have meant many things, from the fact that she didn't appreciate his flippancy to a general abhorrence of his nearness. If he were a gambling man he would bet five-to-one on the latter. "Good morning, Hannah," he said politely. "Sleep well?"

She seemed startled that he spoke to her. She broke eye contact, her gaze darting around as though seeking a safer harbor. Several heartbeats later, she met his eyes again. "I slept fine, thanks." Her lips curved in a brief, pseudo-smile. "Apparently you did, too."

He could fake cordiality as well as the next faker, and cocked a crooked grin. "Like a dead man," he said, taunting her with the reminder of her threat. "Our moonlight swim did it. I went right to sleep—afterward." He winked, rewarded for his audacity by the widening of her eyes. Sexual innuendo often had that effect.

She swallowed, opened her mouth, but nothing came out.

"You went swimming?" Joan asked.

"Not—on purpose." Hannah set the sorghum down and shifted her attention to Joan, then to Deacon. "I—I took out the rowboat. It started leaking, and—well, I guess I screamed or something, because suddenly…" She appeared to have as much trouble saying his name as she did looking at him. Peering askance in his direction, she finally managed. "Roth showed up and sort of—helped—a little." Her cheeks flamed a troubling shade of pink.

"Please," Roth goaded, struggling to hide his frustration. "Such praise. You're embarrassing me."

She gave him a quelling look.

"Can't you swim?" Deacon asked.

Hannah cast her eyes down, staring at her plate for a second before shaking her head. "Not too well."

"Gracious." Joan pressed her hands to her face in a show of alarm. "How frightened you must have been out there in that sinking boat." She reached over and patted Hannah's arm. "That horrible piece of junk. I should have gotten rid of it long ago." She lifted her gaze to Roth. "How very heroic of you, dear boy."

"Yes," Deacon said. "Hannah was fortunate you were there."
An infinitesimal frown line between his eyebrows telegraphed
a touch of jealousy, or possibly merely official concern. He
shifted his attention to Hannah. "It's not a good idea to swim
alone, especially after dark."

"I suppose not." Hannah smiled at Deacon, her expression
exhibiting bashful unease. "I wasn't technically swimming."

"Technically she was drowning," Roth said.

"I was *boating!*" She glared at Roth.

"My mistake." Roth grinned, actually feeling it. There was
that charming spunk he admired, however prickly it might be.
"When I got there she was *boating* to the bottom of the lake."

Hannah heaved a guttural sigh that had all the earmarks of an
oath. "What do you want? A gold star for lifesaving?" she asked.
"Even better, your name in the paper with a huge headline that
reads Roth Jerric Saves Life Of Mediocre Ex-employee?"

Pressing her palms down hard on the tabletop she shoved
up. "I'll see what I can do for your bloated ego while I'm in
Grove." She moved her chair back with the squawk of wood
against wood and walked around the table to stand beside the
sheriff. "Deacon offered to escort me while I do some shop-
ping." She lay a hand on his shoulder, which drew the officer's
gaze. Apparently he wasn't expecting her touch. "Whenever
you're ready, Deacon." Her impatient tone made it clear she
wanted to leave *now.*

He lay his fork on the plate beside a half-eaten stack of pancakes. With a game smile, he removed the napkin from his lap
and placed it on the tabletop. "I'm ready."

She smirked in Roth's direction. "I'm afraid we'll have to
reschedule that swimming lesson," she said. "How does *never*
sound to you?"

Roth eyed her solemnly, then shrugged for show. Inside he
was far from apathetic. Evidently some part of him had been
looking forward to those lessons. "Whatever floats your boat,

sweetheart." He made sure his grin was as caustic as his tone. "But we've both seen what happens when nothing does."

Her smirk faded. "Come on, Deacon." She reached down and grasped his hand, only then breaking eye contact. "You're so thoughtful to offer to show me around Grove."

"My pleasure." Deacon stood and smiled in her direction. Roth wondered if his vague squint meant that he sensed that her eagerness was more show than sincere. Or was that mere wishful thinking? Something about the woman made Roth's judgment go off the rails more often than he liked.

Maybe her interest in the sheriff was genuine and it was her antagonism for Roth and her need to put distance between them that made her hasty rush to Deacon's side seem oversold and artificial. Roth assumed Deacon felt genuine affection for Hannah, or he wouldn't show up at the crack of dawn every day, not even for Joan's pancakes. From the look of things, Joan's manipulations were working.

"Thanks for breakfast," Deacon said to his hostess. With a nod toward Mona, then Roth, he took Hannah's elbow and accompanied her from the inn.

Roth gritted his teeth and tried to concentrate on cutting out a wedge of pancake. Why did Hannah's contempt for him have to gnaw at him so? Why did he care if the handsome sheriff squired her to Grove, or carried her packages while she shopped, or if, right now, they were tearing off their clothes and getting it on in the back seat of the cop car?

Why, jackass? he growled inwardly, *Damn me if I know why!*

Hannah enjoyed Deacon's company. She watched other women in Grove as they passed and could tell many of them wished they were in her place. He was certainly a major catch, and would have been even in a big city. But in a small town like Grove, or Jay, the county seat where his office was, he was absolute gold. She wished she could fall madly in love with him.

But darn her hide, she seemed to be suffering from an incurable thing for Roth Jerric.

Well, doctor heal thy self, she insisted to herself. She and Deacon sat at a booth in a homespun hamburger place of plain, brown tables and booths. The food was plain, too, hamburgers and sandwiches, but it was tasty. Friendly folks made it a point to stop by their table and say hello to their genial, good-looking sheriff.

A few of the women shot daggers at Hannah with their eyes while they smiled a greeting. Hannah acknowledged those stares with amiable grace. She didn't feel like gloating over her good fortune, since her heart seemed determined to pine for someone else—someone without one-tenth the admirable attributes of Sheriff Deacon Vance.

"Would you like dessert?" he asked, drawing her from her musings. "Today there's chocolate or peach pie and several flavors of ice cream."

Hannah smiled. "Anything fat and sugar free?"

He chuckled. "Yeah. Water."

She lay her napkin beside her plate, sobering at the word. "I think I've had enough water lately." When she met his gaze again, she caught his wince. "Is something wrong?"

He shook his head. "It's just that I've recovered several drowning victims from the lake." He leaned forward, placing his forearms on the table. His fingertips were very close to her hand resting on her napkin. "I don't like to think of recovering your..." He didn't finish that sentence. They both understood.

"That late night boat ride was stupid of me," she said.

He slid his hand to take hers, squeezing. "You don't strike me as a stupid woman, Hannah. Why did you do that?"

He knew how to hit the nail on the head with his questions. She smiled sheepishly. "Interrogate much?"

He grinned, but it didn't reach his eyes. "I didn't mean to put you on the spot."

She allowed him to hold her hand. It was a nice hand, large and long-fingered. For a man with such a physical job he had well-kept, neatly trimmed nails. Not manicure-perfect, but neat, manly. She liked his hands. They looked strong, yet he held her fingers gently, as though sensitive to her feelings. Not too firm, not too light, but just the right amount of contact for her to feel comfortable. She wondered how many local woman had thrilled from the touch of those hands.

With a smile that was real, she shook her head to reassure him. "I don't feel like I'm on the spot," she said. "Not really. It's just that I get the feeling from your question that you gathered my decision to go out in that rowboat was because I was upset or restless or something, which is true. I was. I'm a bit— I mean, I have a tendency to be hasty."

"Spontaneity can be a good thing. My wife…" He faltered, lost his smile. "My late wife was a spontaneous soul." His smile returned as he recalled her. "It was one of her most endearing qualities."

Though he did a good job of masking his pain, Hannah saw it in the depths of his eyes, heard it in the slight tightening of his voice. "There are times when I don't prize that quality in myself. Like last night, for instance."

He squeezed her hand, a friendly gesture. "People like me, stodgy, stick-in-the-mud predictable types, admire it."

She placed her free hand over his holding hers. "I'll tell you a secret, Deacon." She leaned toward him, whispering, "You're not stodgy, and people like me admire predictability. People like you are the rock that people like me need. We attach our kitelike personalities to your rocklike ones, so we can dip and bob in the gusty winds of our whims, knowing we won't get snagged in a tree, because we're safe as long as we're fastened to that stable rock."

His eyes softened and the deep pain seemed to diminish. "Jennifer used to say something very much like that."

"She was a lucky woman, and she knew it."

He glanced away and stared out the window. After a moment, he met her eyes again. "Thank you."

Hannah squeezed his hand affectionately, then withdrew hers. "I've taken up enough of your day, Sheriff. Didn't you say you had a one o'clock appointment in your office in Jay?"

He nodded then lifted his hand from hers to check his watch. "I'll just have enough time to get you back to the inn before my meeting."

"I appreciate all you've done." She slid from the booth.

"My pleasure." He took her arm. "So, what was it that upset you so much you felt the need to go rowing in the middle of the night?"

She hiked her handbag to her shoulder and avoided eye contact. She'd hoped that subject was closed. "Oh, let's just say I haven't found my nice, safe rock."

"I see." He held the door open as they exited.

Once in the patrol car, they rode along in companionable silence for a time, then he said, "I thought it might have something to do with Roth Jerric."

Hannah was so startled by the mention of Roth's name she couldn't find her voice for several seconds. She looked at Deacon. "Why—why would you think that?"

He shifted to glance at her as he rounded a curve in the blacktop road, rising and dipping across the hilly woodland. "Just a hunch."

"Actually I don't like the man much. He's trying to steal Joan's property out from under her."

"I'm afraid somebody will, if things don't turn around," he said thoughtfully. "She owes a lot of back taxes. Another year, and the property will be scheduled for a Sheriff's auction." He pursed his lips. "I don't look forward to that. She's a friend, and turning her out of her house is the last thing I want to do."

"Actually, Roth paid her back taxes."

Deacon glanced at her. "Really?"

"I told you. He's out to steal her property right out from under her. But I won't let him. I'm going to help turn things around for her," she said, reaffirming her decision out loud. She was a firm believer that the more something was declared aloud, the truer it became.

"Oh?" He glanced her way.

"I need a job and she needs a financial manager."

"That would be good, if you could help her. She does love that place."

"And Roth won't be free to turn the property into gated housing, condos and a marina, and Joan won't have to move into some blah condominium that has no heart or charm."

"Condominium?"

"That's what Roth says he'll do for her—give her some boring condo."

"You mean he'd *give* her housing?"

"Yes," she said. "But as *you* pointed out, she loves her home and she wants to live out her life there."

"Hmm."

His noncommittal response bothered Hannah. It was as though he didn't think some sterile condo was all that bad. "Well?"

"I wish you luck." He glanced her way. "But truth be told, turning her financial situation around is a long shot. If Roth's plan is to give her a condo, it's damn generous."

Hannah frowned. Were all men devoid of sentiment? "I think it's heartless."

After a moment, Deacon chuckled. "I think I understand."

"Good." She crossed her arms, relieved. "I was afraid for a second you sided with Roth."

"I wasn't talking about the condominium."

She peered his way, concerned. She didn't have a good feeling about this. "Then what were you talking about?"

"Your outing on the lake."

She quickly looked away to stare out the window. She definitely didn't have a good feeling about this. She recognized where they were. The inn was mere minutes away. That was lucky, because she didn't like the direction of this conversation.

"You're attracted to Roth, and you don't want to be."

"That's absurd," she said, too quickly.

He turned onto the inn's gravel driveway. "Is it?"

"Absolutely." She kept her eyes glued on the scenery. The church ruins came into view. She concentrated on that. There was the bench, the wall, the arched opening where the window used to be.

The squad car came to a halt with a gravelly crunch. "Here we are," he said.

"Mmm-hmm." She nodded. "Thanks for everything." With effort, she faced him.

"Happy to do it." He smiled cordially. "I'll get your packages out of the trunk."

"Thanks." Not wanting him to feel the need to open her door, she grabbed the handle and let herself out. As she walked around to meet Deacon beside the trunk, she fidgeted with her handbag strap, tugged on her cotton tank top. He pulled several bags from the trunk and set them on the gravel, then surprised her by taking her chin in his fingers. "Let's try a little experiment."

Before she could ask him what he meant, he kissed her, the experience tingly and pleasant. He kissed very well, especially considering the fact that he wasn't putting his heart into it. She recalled the pain of loss in his eyes when he spoke of his late wife, and knew he wasn't ready for a relationship. So why the kiss?

Raising his mouth from hers, he gazed into her eyes. "Maybe there's something to Joan's blue moon theory, after all."

She stared, the pleasant tingle in her lips dying a quick death. "What do you mean?" She feared she knew but she refused to accept it.

"Come now, Hannah," he said with a slight upturn of his lips. "We've already determined you're not a stupid woman." He lifted the packages and held them out for her to take. "Sometimes an outsider can see things clearer than those close to a situation. And that kiss just now had 'I'm taken' all over it."

She accepted the packages hardly registering what she was doing. "Please, don't suggest that being caught in the light of that blue moon with Roth Jerric, through a hole in a crumbling wall, has any merit, because I told you, I don't even *like* the man."

"I know what you told me," he said. "But I also witnessed your little performance at breakfast."

"What little performance?" Had Deacon recognized the fear behind her flap with Roth?

"From what I gathered, Roth saved your life." He grazed her jutted chin with a finger. "Rather than show gratitude, you acted like he kicked your dog. That doesn't make sense, unless you're fighting an attraction for him."

"That's absur—"

"Then you cozied up to me," he went on, undeterred by her objection. "Not that I minded, but we both know who that little charade was for, and it wasn't me."

Disconcerted, she cleared her throat. Deacon Vance was an insightful man. "I repeat, I don't like Roth Jerric." That was the *truth*—as she wanted the truth to be. "How many different ways must I say it?"

"Why say it at all?" He brushed a stray wisp of hair behind her ear. "He seems like a decent guy."

"Well, he's not. He's opinionated, insensitive and arrogant." Bitterness sharpened her tone. "For your information, he called me mediocre." She didn't know why she blurted that out. Was she worried her denials of an attraction for the man needed buttressing?

Deacon's expression showed disbelief. "He didn't call you mediocre. I can't believe that."

"He *did!*" she shot back, though indebted to him for his incredulity.

Deacon frowned in thought. "He actually said to you, 'Hannah, I think you're mediocre'?"

She grew annoyed. Why must he refuse to take her declaration at face value? "He didn't say it to me directly. But that doesn't mean he didn't say it."

"Then, someone told you he said it?" Deacon asked.

"No, I overheard somebody say he said it."

"That's not exactly indisputable evidence." Deacon surveyed her solemnly but kindly. "I don't get the sense he thinks anything of the kind about you."

"That's not exactly indisputable evidence, either." She struggled to maintain an even tone. "No offense."

He grinned. "None taken." Shutting the trunk, he went on, "Did you confront him?"

"No," she said. "Of course not."

"Why not?"

His gaze had not wavered from hers. She felt intimidated by both the intensity of his look and his attachment to the subject. "Let's say I had it on good authority he thought I was a mediocre employee and leave it at that. Why humiliate myself with a face-to-face?" she demanded with a rush of irritation. "I knew my career at Jerric Oil was dead, so I quit."

"You worked for him at the time?"

"Stop interrogating me." She felt the beginnings of a headache. "It's water under the bridge. Let it go."

"I'm sorry." He looked concerned. "I didn't mean to upset you, but I can't imagine anyone saying that about you."

"Thanks for that, anyway." The day had grown hot and humid, the sky a cloudless, burning blue. Somehow Deacon managed to look unwrinkled and cool, his brown uniform crisp and spotless. She felt sticky, fretful and rumpled. Taking a deep breath, she forgave him, for both his meddling and his ability to look perfect even in ninety-degree heat.

"Ask him point-blank," Deacon said.

"Ask who what?"

"Ask Roth if he said you were mediocre."

"I thought we'd finished with that subject."

"Ask him."

"Would you get off it?" she cried. "Besides, he'd lie."

Deacon shook his head. "No, he wouldn't."

"Oh, and you know this for a fact?" Her tone dripped with mockery. "How is it you're so all-knowing?"

"Just lucky, I guess." He smiled, unfazed. "Trust me on this."

His smile had its effect. Against her will, she smiled back, though not as wholeheartedly. "Get out of here, you busybody."

Surprising her, he took her gently into his arms and brushed her cheek with a kiss. "Promise me you'll ask," he whispered. "I have a feeling you're closer to finding your rock than you care to admit."

He stepped back, his hands sliding to her forearms. "And you might think about taking him up on those swimming lessons." Before relinquishing her completely, he squeezed her arms with affection.

The crunch of boots telegraphed his trek to the driver's side of the squad car. His door closed with a boom, and the engine growled to life.

Somehow, Hannah couldn't move. Had he actually had the audacity to suggest Roth Jerric was her rock? Ridiculous! What nerve! She would have to reconsider how insightful she thought the sheriff was considering *that* fantastic suggestion.

"You might want to move out of the way," a masculine voice called.

Still dumbfounded, she slowly turned toward the sound.

On the far side of the inn, Roth came out of the shadow of

a clump of trees. At that distance he couldn't have heard their conversation. Thank goodness for that. "The car." Roth indicated the sheriff's vehicle.

Belatedly she came out of her daze. "Oh…" She stepped aside.

After maneuvering to turn around in the driveway, Deacon waved a farewell.

"Did you have a nice time?" Roth asked as the squad car drove out of sight.

"Yes." She nodded. "I did." That wasn't a lie. For the most part, she did have fun. Only the last minute or two became troubling.

"I gathered."

She stared at him, confused.

He took her packages. "The kisses." He watched her, his expression unreadable. "That usually means things went well."

She flushed, too aware of his scrutiny. Roth Jerric was *not* her rock. Deacon might be a fine sheriff, but he was a rotten judge of rocks. "Well, yes, it's true. I had a terrific time—with *Deacon*." Why she decided she needed to add the sheriff's name she didn't know. Maybe to underscore the fact that Roth was not the be-all and end-all of male attractiveness. She certainly wanted that to be the truth. Shifting toward the inn, she trudged away, putting real estate between them. "Yes, Deacon and I had an absolutely *terrific* time."

CHAPTER NINE

"Do YOU mind if I ask a question?" Roth called out as she hurried off.

Hannah made a pained face, thinking, *Can't you just carry my packages and let me walk away from you?* Reluctantly she put off her getaway and turned around. "A question?"

He caught up in two strides. "You've made a couple of references to my thinking you're mediocre. The latest was this morning," he said. "I'd like to know where that's coming from."

Talk about weird coincidences. Not five minutes ago, Deacon told her to ask Roth point-blank about it, and here he was, bringing it up himself. Which was strange, considering calling an employee mediocre should be memorable. She stared at him, her festering resentment boiling to the surface. "You know exactly where it's coming from."

He shook his head, as though frustrated. "That's what I mean. Cryptic comments like that." Aggravation shadowed his eyes. "*Damn it,* I have no idea where it's coming from."

He stood there, serious and silent, waiting. She hated the way he made her pulse rate pick up. She reminded herself of her mistake with Milo. She needed to kill the attraction she felt for Roth, a dominant alpha male if ever there was one. "Are you standing there with your bare face hanging out, telling me you did *not* discuss me with Milo?" She took a deep breath before grimly going on. "And are you suggesting you did *not* tell him I was a mediocre employee?"

His gaze steady, he remained closemouthed for a moment, the expression on his face growing more tense by the second. Finally he said, "Not only am I suggesting I said no such thing, I'm stating it in no uncertain terms." She detected a touch of anger in his voice. "Milo told you I did?"

She nodded, then shook her head. The vehemence of his denial came as a shock, confusing her.

"Well, which is it, yes or no?"

"It's yes. No, I mean—uh…I overheard him tell several people you said it, and how he agreed with your assessment."

A sound issued up from Roth's throat, a growl-like noise. "Milo is an excellent lawyer, but an ass of a human being." He mouthed a curse, looking past her toward the lake. His jaw worked, the muscles in his cheeks bunching, indicating high agitation. After a moment, he refocused on her. "That's why you quit?"

She nodded, struck mute by the force of his disgust over Milo's abominable behavior. He was so handsome, with those high cheekbones, piercing blue eyes, that powerful body. Anger on her behalf magnified his attractiveness tenfold.

Lord, save me from collapsing at his feet in a trembly heap of desire. She reminded herself sternly that he might be angry on her behalf now, but if she allowed herself to succumb to her attraction, what about the times in the future when they disagreed? She wouldn't have a chance. By the sheer intensity of his personality, he held the power to grind her wants and needs to dust. *Whoa, girl, don't get ahead of yourself. One sexual encounter, no matter how extraordinary, does not make a relationship.*

She could only stand and watch as emotions ebbed and flowed across his face. At last, his annoyance faded. "Then the problem's solved," he said.

His remark didn't compute. "What problem?"

He held out his arms in an all-encompassing gesture, her bags dangling from his fists. "You can come back. Everybody knows Milo is an egocentric blowhard. Half of what he says about women is exaggeration and the other half pure fiction."

"*I* didn't know any such thing."

"Well, the men know." He shook his head. "Look, I can understand why you believed your career might not thrive in an atmosphere where your boss thought you were mediocre. But since it isn't true, and apparently only you gave Milo's idiotic story any credence, you can come back."

"Come back?" she asked, in disbelief. "You don't mean to Jerric Oil?"

"Of course I do."

She stared, amazed that he could even suggest such a thing. "Are you insane?"

His expression indicated he didn't understand. "I beg your pardon?"

Apparently he didn't think a grateful ex-employee who'd just been offered her job back would suggest he was out of his mind. "I can't come back to work for you."

"Why? I just said—"

"I know what you said," she interrupted. "And I said that's insane. We've…" Her mind's eye conjured up visions of the two of them making love in the shower, the sweet, wild passion they shared. How did she say all that without actually saying it. "We've—done things…" Her heart beating furiously, she shook her head. "We can't work together. Especially not with you as my boss. I wouldn't be comfortable." Clearly he had no problem with it. Apparently the impetuous beauty of their lovemaking meant little to him and was easily shrugged off.

He watched her, his brow as creased as ever. "I can give you the career you want," he said, tension once again evident in his tone.

"I don't want you to give me anything," she said. "I am capable of making my own successes."

He lifted an eyebrow and chuckled deep in his chest, a sardonic, dubious sound. "And capable of making your own failures, it seems, if you insist on attaching yourself to the fate of the Blue Moon Inn."

"I do insist," she said, pricked by his assumption that she would fail.

Now it was his turn to look incredulous. "You can't be serious." His voice had grown sharp.

"Oh, yes. And since you *say* you don't think I'm mediocre, then you can plan on *not* stealing Joan's property for a pittance."

"Turning this place around will take more than mere competence," he said. "It will take a magician."

Her outrage overrode the dark spell of his charisma. She felt her blood soar to the roots of her hair. Lifting her arms she wagged her fingers, burlesquing sleight-of-hand. "Well, then, *Abra—freaking—cadabra!*"

Pivoting away, she trudged toward the inn, praying that taking on Joan's struggling business hadn't been biting off more than she could chew. Was she a fool? She'd just turned down an opportunity for an awesome career. *No, no, Hannah,* she argued silently. *You had to. How could you stand seeing him every day? How could you go to meetings with him, look at him simply as your boss—remembering his touch, his taste, knowing he was kissing other women, holding them, making love…*

She shook herself. Even if—*when*—she rid herself of the unwanted attraction she felt, working for him was no longer an option. And it wasn't just because of what had gone on between them. Big corporations and the petty superficiality of office politics weren't for her. Jerric Oil taught her that her nature was better suited to a small, familylike work environment. The Blue Moon Inn was certainly that.

The fact that it even mattered to her that Roth really didn't think of her as mediocre unsettled her. She didn't need his stamp of approval. Even so, she found herself walking a little taller than she had in over a month.

It was possible she could fail in her attempt to save the Blue Moon Inn. But if she did, it wouldn't be because she was mediocre. It would be because the cause was hopeless. She winced. *No negative thinking, Hannah. Joan's peace of mind and happiness rest squarely on your shoulders now.*

You must not fail.

Agitated and unsure why, Hannah paced around her room. While she was gone that morning with Deacon, Roth had once again engaged Joan in conversation about his plans for her property. Again, he detailed his desire to set her up in a condo. Joan was in a state of high anxiety when Hannah walked into the house. For a whole minute and a half before Joan flung herself into Hannah's arms, weeping, she'd felt slightly less antagonistic toward Roth. A *whole* minute and a half.

After managing to calm her hostess by promising that her command of finance management would have the inn turning a profit within the year, she escaped to her room to shower where she could panic in private. How did anyone turn a profit on a musty, out-of-the-way inn with only four guest rooms and no money to advertise or spruce up the place? She stood under the water for a long time. No immediate, miraculous answer came to her. Well, she'd just have to think more on it. Something would come to her. It had to.

Several minutes later, she cinched up the sash on her robe and took another trek around her room, thinking, worrying. She ran both hands through her hair, still damp from her shower. "What to do? What to do?" she mumbled. As she turned toward the balcony door, her head bowed in thought, she heard a thud, as though something had hit the window. She knew that sound. A bird had flown into the glass.

Jerking up her head, she saw a robin fall to the balcony

deck. "Oh!" She froze in indecision. What should she do? Should she leave it alone or check on it? At least on the balcony it wasn't in danger of being pounced on by a passing cat. "Maybe just leave it," she thought aloud. "Surely it will recover in a minute."

The bird's plight displaced her other worries. All she could think about now was that unconscious little robin. It didn't move, but a breeze fluttered a few of its downy, red breast feathers. She anxiously nibbled at a fingernail, watching for signs of life. "Come on, little guy. Wake up." It had probably only been a couple of minutes, but it seemed like forever.

Movement off to the side startled her, then Roth came into view. She watched as he scooped up the bird. Alarm gripped her as visions of him flinging the helpless creature off the balcony filled her head. She instinctively started toward the door.

Just as she was about to lay her hand on the doorknob, he began to stroke the bird. She stilled, lifted her attention to his face, his eyes, amazed to see a glimmer of concern there. He shifted, angling away. She could no longer see his face or his actions, but she knew he had no plans to hurl the bird over the railing.

He was helping it, actually caring for it. Soundlessly she turned the knob and cracked open the door. To her surprise she could hear him murmuring to the bird. She couldn't make out what he said, but the soothing tones further reassured her about his motives. Movement in his right arm and shoulder told her he continued to stroke the bird. And though she couldn't hear his words, she guessed he murmured encouragements. Who would have thought Roth, of all people, would care about one little bird?

After a moment she watched the robin flutter to the rail, then fly up and away. She smiled, not only because she was relieved to see that it was okay, but because Roth's gentleness touched her. Memories rushed back of the way he looked with Joan's dog after he spent the night searching for it. That smudged cheek, the glisten of emotion in his eyes, emotion he resented even feeling.

A second later she found herself on the balcony. Roth rested his hands on the railing, no doubt to watch the bird disappear into the distance. She joined him. Neither spoke, though she knew he was aware of her presence. That quiet moment was somehow special for her. She knew she wouldn't soon forget how he looked with the robin. His expression exhibited a sober kinship with the bird's pain that was immensely poignant and endearing. Impulsively she touched his hand that rested on the rail. "I had no idea you could be so—so *human.*"

Her remark drew his narrowed gaze. Even in the sultry afternoon heat, his narrowed stare was chilling. "No?" After a moment, he lifted his hand away from hers to run his fingers lightly across her ear and through her damp hair. "I thought we shared a few very human moments."

His light touch set her skin to tingling. The murmured reminder of their lovemaking left her dazed and speechless.

Before she recovered herself, he was gone.

So human? Back inside his room, Roth came to a halt, seeing nothing. Hannah's remark bothered him. But his own reply bothered him more. Why had he said what he'd said? *I thought we shared a few very human moments.* Yes, he'd felt more alive. Yes, he'd been more open with her, unguarded, even a little vulnerable. But he hadn't been happy about it. He prided himself on his ability to control his emotional impulses, aware how dangerous they could be. In the process, his life became mechanical, and, yes, he had to admit it—in many ways his life had also become empty.

For the first time he experienced doubts about the wisdom of his choice. Was the trade-off worth it? He had returned to his old family home to reenergize, reevaluate and renew himself. Did that renewal mean he must rehumanize, too?

He looked around his room. It had been his sister's when the house belonged to his family. He recalled how it looked all those years ago. Plain, pine furniture his dad made, the crazy quilt that covered the bed, hand-sewn by his mother from fabric scraps.

No wallpaper covered the walls then. His parents had let him and his sister, Gracie, pick the paint colors for their bedrooms. Gracie's room became a blinding orange. He experienced a rush of soft emotion, disquieting yet galvanizing. That horrible orange color seemed as bright and cheerful as Gracie's laughter. He hadn't thought about that in a long time, and since Gracie's move to California with her computer guru husband, he hadn't heard her infectious laughter in years, hardly knew his nephews, Greg and Reed. In the black stillness of his mind the memory of Gracie's laugh came back to him, pure and clear. The recollection brought a wry smile to his face and a dull ache in his chest.

His old family home held a lot of memories, happy and sad. Since his arrival he'd purposely avoided thinking about the past. Memories tended to be emotional quagmires. But now they rushed into his mind like flood waters over a broken dam.

He sat down heavily on his bed with the weight of them. They battered his defenses with great ferocity, but his strength of will kept them at bay. He had no intention of waxing nostalgic over a few childish flashbacks or a pile of bricks.

Money could be made here. Big money. Acquiring the property only required a little time and a pitifully small amount of capital. Child's play. As Delaware county was one of the fastest growing in population in the country—all those moneyed baby boomers retiring to their scenic lake homes—he could reap another vast fortune with practically no effort.

Just because Joan was a mawkishly sentimental creature too stubborn for her own good, it didn't mean she had to live out her life breaking her back cleaning and cooking in a dilapidated old house. Her short-sighted thinking didn't allow her to see how his plans benefited her, so he would save her from herself. It was a win-win deal when viewed logically.

"Logically?" he muttered. Why did the word suddenly have a hollow sound? "What's wrong with you, Jerric? Don't let a pair of eyes, the touch of a hand and a whispered homage to humanness derail you. You know what to do," he ground out. "Don't start second-guessing yourself." He hunched forward to hold his head in his hands.

So if he knew what to do, why the mental blur? Why did he feel sick and drained. Maybe he had a touch of the flu. He lay back on the bed to stare at the ceiling. His head throbbed. His limbs felt leaden. Even his bones ached. "Maybe it's something I ate." He squeezed his eyes shut. *Or maybe you're remembering what it feels like to be human,* a bothersome voice whispered.

"Oh, shut up." He threw an arm across his eyes. The sooner he reburied his flawed, vulnerable self, the better.

CHAPTER TEN

HANNAH dressed hurriedly and dashed downstairs to help Joan prepare supper. Activity of any kind was better than standing alone on that balcony tingling from Roth's touch and smarting from his offhand reminder of what they had shared.

She was glad to hear Joan humming as she entered the kitchen. Apparently her pep talk had done its job. She only wished she felt as secure in her ability to save the inn as Joan did. The older woman turned at the sound of Hannah's approach. She smiled and waved her potato peeler. "Hello, dear." She gave Hannah an approving inspection. "You look fresh as a daisy in that pretty sundress. Pink is definitely your color."

Hannah smiled her thanks. "It's cool."

Joan nodded, understanding. "I'm sorry the air-conditioning isn't running any better than it is. But at least it's eighty in here, not ninety-six, like it is outside."

"True." Hannah looked around. The kitchen was as neat as ever and little Missy Mis was asleep on her rug in an out of the way corner. Sitting in front of Joan on the green-tiled countertop was a big, gray pottery bowl full of peeled potatoes, enough for dinner. "What do you need me to do?"

"Cut up these spuds for boiling, and I'll get started on the peach pie's crust."

Hannah couldn't help but laugh. "One more piece of your

delicious peach pie, and I won't be able to squeeze into my jeans."

"Don't be silly." Joan bustled around getting the ingredients for her crust. "You young women today are too thin. You could afford to put on a few pounds."

Hannah plucked a paring knife from a drawer and began to cut a raw potato into cubes on the old cutting board. "Ah, but I can't afford new jeans." She bit her tongue, annoyed with herself. *Hannah, you shouldn't have brought up your financial situation.* She didn't care to get into the discussion about saving the inn right now. She was too emotionally overwrought. Her brain was all but mush. Roth's touch could do that kind of damage.

Joan's smile didn't dim. "That's going to change, once you start this place making money."

Hannah smiled weakly and floundered for another topic. "Um, are these pieces about right?" She held up a chunk of potato.

"Perfect," Joan said. "I've set out a pot. When you've cut up them all, cover them with water and turn on the burner real low."

"Got it."

"So, how was this morning with dear Deacon?"

Hannah almost sliced her finger. Another topic she would have preferred to avoid. Had that only been today? It seemed like forever ago. "Uh, fine."

"Isn't he the most darling man alive?"

"I wouldn't be surprised." She focused on the potatoes, cutting them up with concentrated preciseness. For a while the only sound in the kitchen was the thud of her knife against the cutting board and the slight grating noise of Joan's flour sifter. When she finished cubing several potatoes, she scooped the chunks into the pot. What subject could she bring up that would distract Joan from her matchmaking? Her mind racing, she grabbed another potato from the bowl. "You know, I've been mulling over ways to advertise the inn, and I was thinking, since you love chat rooms so much, and have so many online friends, we could—"

"Wonderful, dear," Joan interrupted. "Did you and Deacon do anything *especially* interesting?"

Hannah was suspicious of Joan's emphasis on the word "especially." It almost sounded like she knew about the kiss in the driveway and assumed the romance had blossomed into the first blush of true love. *If only!* How she wished she could say it were true. Deacon was quite a man.

"Um, well…" Hannah sighed deep and long. Why beat about the bush? Setting her knife on the cutting block, she faced Joan. "To be honest…" She shook her head, searching for the right words. "Deacon is still very much in love with his late wife, which is really okay, because I'm not in the market for a relationship right now." In her head, that was true. Too bad her heart silently added…*except for one brainless infatuation with a bully whose slightest touch scorches my very soul.*

"I don't believe that," Joan said. She set the sifter on the counter with such force a cloud of white billowed up. "Not after what *I* saw."

Her cagey tone made it clear Hannah was right in her suspicion. Joan had been peeking when the driveway kiss took place. She should have known no self-respecting matchmaker would let an opportunity slip by to spy on the matched couple. She felt her face go hot. Picking up the knife, she went back to cutting. "Yes, we did kiss, but it was an experiment—on Deacon's part."

"An experiment in love." Joan sounded delighted. "You two made such a sweet couple out there kissing like lovebirds."

Hannah worked at keeping calm. It wouldn't do to get upset while using a knife. "No, it was an experiment that—that failed."

After a brief pause, long enough for Joan's smile to die, she said, "I don't understand."

Hannah glanced away from her hostess. "He said…" She had to let the sentence trail off, since she didn't dare repeat what he said about her "being taken." She didn't dare say that out loud. She sidestepped by lying. "He said he could only be my friend." She faced Joan. "What you saw was a 'thanks but no thanks' kiss." That last part came pretty close to the truth.

Joan's face clouded. "I can't believe it. He told me he was attracted to you."

Joan had actually spoken to Deacon about her? Hannah wished she were dead. "Well, I'm flattered, naturally, that he would say such a thing. But you can be attracted to a person, and it can still be the wrong time for anything to come of it." She placed a hand on Joan's. "What you tried to do for Deacon, and for me, was very sweet. And one day, a woman will come along who attracts him to the extent that he can let go of his devotion to his dead wife. I envy that woman, because she'll be very lucky. But it's not me. He's not ready. And—and neither am I." She patted Joan's hand, then picked up the knife and began to cut up the remaining potatoes. "Honestly, Joan, I never intend to be dependent on any man, or be any man's arm candy—ever again." Chopping, unable to look at Joan's face, she went on gravely, "I came here to get my self-confidence back so I could go out and kick some corporate ass." She managed a quaking smile at that thought.

How things had changed in a little over a week. She trained her smile on Joan. "I have begun to regain my confidence, and I've gained insight into myself. I know now that I don't want to work for a big company." She nodded to certify her resolve. "You helped me do that. And that's far from a small thing." She dumped the last of the potato chunks into the pot and carried it to the sink to add water. "You should be proud."

After covering the potatoes with water, Hannah moved the pot to the stove. Joan hadn't spoken, which was unlike her. Curious, Hannah faced the older woman. Her expression seemed too bleak for all the complimentary things Hannah had said. "What's wrong, Joan?"

Her hostess smiled, a melancholy effort. "You mustn't be bitter toward men, dear, simply because you've had a bad experience or two."

"I'm not bitter toward men," Hannah said, surprised by Joan's suggestion.

"I think you are. Before I sent you that coupon for your free two-week vacation, we chatted in the chat room about your experience at your last job and about your parents' divorce. Remember?"

Hannah did. "Okay, I may have sounded a little..." She searched for the right word.

"Bitter," Joan said. She began to cut shortening into the flour. "It's wonderful to be independent, Hannah. I, too, was an independent lass." She got that faraway look in her eyes as she always did when she thought of her late husband. "I was quite progressive for my day. I didn't need a mate for my happiness." She laughed at the memory. "I was so young, so full of myself and violently protective of my freedom." She met Hannah's gaze. "You see, I came from a family in which my father had been dictatorial, perhaps much like your father. I vowed, when I left home, I would never let a man dominate or boss me."

She fingered the pastry cutter absently. "And no man ever did. But not because I avoided a relationship, but because my darling Dur was my other half, my soul mate. I could have painted him with the same brush as my father, pushed him away out of fear or resentment or stubbornness. But fortunately, I allowed a deeper wisdom within myself to be heard. *Trust this man,* it whispered. *Trust this feeling that, as yet, has no name.*" She smiled, began to work again. "I did, Hannah. I trusted something deep inside me that I did not wholly understand or even believe, at first. It was that indefinable feeling, that small voice, and then Dur's thoughtful behavior that brought me to the truth.

"Dur was not my arrogant, blustering father in another guise. Dur was my ally, my lover, my balance. He was my laughter when I had only tears, my boldness when I was shy and my light when I stumbled in the darkness." Her expression held stunning conviction. At that moment Hannah saw Joan as the young, ardent, freethinker she had been when she met her husband. Witnessing this side of her, Hannah admired her hostess more than ever, redoubling her commitment to help her out of her financial straits.

"A truly blissful mate will not wish to dominate or bully you, dear," Joan went on. "He will be your bulwark to lean on, and for whom you will be the same. Yes, for those times when he needs your strength, you will find deep wells of it within yourself to give him, because that is what you want—for him—more than life itself." She nodded, reassuringly. "Don't close yourself up so much that you won't recognize your other half when he appears. I can think of no more desolate existence than to find your soul's mate and then repulse him out of blind bitterness or foolish hardheadedness."

Hannah was touched by Joan's words. She felt tears well and blinked them back. "I'll try," she said, her voice rusty with emotion. She hugged the older woman. "Thanks."

Joan hugged back, patting Hannah's shoulder. "Though Ross and I have our differences, I fancy he truly is your proper mate, after all."

Hannah backed out of the hug, her mood veering from warm and fuzzy to stricken. "What?"

Joan went back to preparing her pie crust. "The blue moon, dear."

"Well, I don't *fancy* any such a thing!"

"Destiny is not always ours to understand."

"But he's controlling and dominant and not a bit like your Dur."

Joan shrugged, looking sympathetic. "Perhaps with you, he would be different."

"Perhaps he'll sprout wings and a halo, too. But I doubt it," Hannah said, sarcastically. "Besides, even if he were different with me, I couldn't love a man who treated people the way he's treated you. Threatening and upsetting you the way he has."

"Are my ears burning?"

Roth's question spun Hannah toward the door. "You should wear a bell so people can have advanced warning that you're coming."

He grinned crookedly though any true pleasantness didn't register in his eyes. "Must be the shoes." He indicated the brown loafers with a wave. "Soft soles. Sorry."

"Hello, Ross," Joan said, her hostess comportment as flawless as ever. "Would you like something? Perhaps a snack to tide you over until dinner?"

"We can't afford to give snacks away—willy-nilly," Hannah said, her expression daring him to ask for something.

He pursed his lips, matching her stare for stare. "Now that I think about it, I am a little hungry."

"Well, then…" Joan looked flustered. "Actually, Hannah," she said in a nearly inaudible aside, "I've always kept an open kitchen for my guests."

"If we're going to put this place on a paying basis that needs to change."

"I'll just rummage through the refrigerator." Roth moved toward it. "To see what tempts me."

Hannah headed him off. Plastering herself against the refrigerator, she flung her arms wide. "Over my dead body."

Standing a foot away, he chuckled. "Don't tempt me, sweetheart."

"Children, children, please." Joan sounded worried, but Hannah didn't take her eyes off Roth. His smile reminded her of a wolf's snarl; his eyes fired sparks that set off a disquieting tingle in the pit of her stomach. The air crackled with electricity. She felt jumpy. Not that she feared he would harm her, but she foolishly dared him to eat something, when he had doubtlessly been passing through the kitchen with no intention of asking for a snack. When would she learn *not* to be so impulsive?

Suddenly it happened—too fast for her to prepare. His hands held her face, his lips claimed hers. The kiss initiated a chain of events. Her heartbeat skyrocketed. She experienced a quiver of delight, then a strange aching in her limbs. Fire surged through her veins, setting off a giddy sense of pleasure.

His mouth moved over hers, hungry, provocative, softly devouring, urging wild responses. She felt drunk and dizzy. Her mind grew numb and she succumbed to the gentle captivity of his lips, returning his kiss with abandon, moaning out her joy.

An instant later the earth tipped precariously on its axis. Disoriented, Hannah found herself clinging to the refrigerator in an effort to remain upright. Roth's hands no longer cupped her face; his lips no longer claimed hers. He towered there, so near, his magnetism as potent as his kiss. Her lips burned. Raw longing raged through her body.

"That should hold me—for a while," he said, his voice guttural and thick.

A heartbeat later, the back door slammed and he was gone.

A knot rose in her throat along with a whispery cry of dismay. Without a mighty force of will, she would have slid to the floor in a heap.

"Mercy!" Joan said.

Hannah had forgotten she and Roth weren't the only two people in the world, let alone the room. She closed her eyes, mortified.

"He certainly is a passionate man," Joan said, sounding awed.

Hannah peered at her hostess, aghast at the very idea. "He's—he's…" She licked her lips, tasting him. She experienced a renewed, wanton rush of desire and bit her lip to quell it. "He's a hard, empty man," she managed breathlessly, "and he's the most grossly *dispassionate* human being on earth."

Joan smiled charitably. "If you say so." She sounded unpersuaded. Shuffling over to Hannah, Joan smoothed a strand of hair off her face. "Never allow him to kiss you passionately, then, dear." She took Hannah's arm and led her to a kitchen bench. "It would kill you."

"You did it again." Roth ran both hands through his hair, astonished at his lack of control around Hannah. He'd actually hauled off and kissed her, in the kitchen, in front of Joan Peterson. What was he thinking? Where was his mind? He breathed a curse, fearing he knew where his mind was, or more importantly where it wasn't. And it wasn't on business. His mind, as well as other less-cerebral parts of him, seemed to have a contrary obsession with a pair of gray-green eyes that sparked with passion. Why he felt an attraction to this spitfire—and here was the most annoying, and strangely ironic part—she made no effort to hide the fact that she disliked him fiercely.

Even knowing that, he kept kissing her. Why? There were plenty of willing females in the world who would be happy with his attention. But no, he went around kissing a woman who threw herself bodily in his way at every turn, be it to buy a failing inn or open a refrigerator door. Of course, on one occasion, she had thrown herself bodily into a sexual encounter with him—gloriously satisfying and impossible to forget. She seemed to hate both herself and him for it. "You're a fool, Jerric," he muttered, rambling in no particular direction. "You don't need this kind of complication."

"Mr. Jerric, you've happened along at exactly the right moment," Mona called from her painting spot in the afternoon shade of the old church ruins. "Come here, please?"

Roth glanced in Mona's direction, surprised he'd wandered

so close to where she painted without noticing. Since he didn't have anything to do at the moment besides berate himself for his rashness, he did as she asked. "Afternoon, Mona." He nodded politely.

She looked him over dourly, tilting her head this way and that. He felt like a prize bull being judged at a state fair. "What can I do for you?" he asked, grateful to have something to take his mind off his preoccupation with Hannah. "Would you like me to get you something cool to drink?"

"No," Mona said. "I never imbibe while my muse is in ascension." She beckoned for him to come closer. "I need your help for a new artistic endeavor."

Considering Mona's penchant for paint throwing, he wondered if his cotton shirt and shorts would survive the day. "Oh?" he asked.

Mona, the sun-dried raisin of a woman, wore a paint-smudged green smock over her tie-dyed tee and frayed and ripped jeans. Her salt and paper hair fell around her thin face in thick, serpentine disarray. It had to be stifling. He wondered how she could stand all that hanging hair and so many layers of clothes in near one hundred degree heat. By contrast, her sun-browned feet were bare except for rubber flip-flops.

She took a paint spattered canvas down from her easel and set it against a nearby tree. To Roth, the art piece depicted yet another very like all her others, a blotchy batch of hues flung from a variety of brushes and found objects cluttered around her feet. He could make out several, a wire whisk, leather belt, several pieces of plastic greenery and one lady's high heel shoe. "Yes, I've had a brainstorm that simply must be explored." She placed a clean, blank canvas on the easel. "My muse howled out 'torso study' and here you are. Extremely providential for us both. You shall be my first torso to be immortalized in oils. Take off your shirt." She waved demonstratively in his direction. "I'll decide about the shorts later."

He couldn't help grinning at her offhand and misguided conceit that he would model in the nude for her. He was no prude and certainly no saint, but for him nudity had a time and place, and it definitely wasn't here and now. "Happy to help." He peeled the shirt off over his head and tossed it across the low branch of a nearby oak. "You should know, I'm very expensive."

Mona examined him with a critical artist's eye. "Interesting." She pointed her brush at his chest, motioning for emphasis. "You have well developed pectorals and marvelous abdominals. You could model professionally."

"I'll keep it in mind," he said, amused.

She nodded with what looked like satisfaction. Tapping her chin with the wooden end of the brush, she added, "Quite nice. Good definition."

"If you think I'll charge less because of your compliments, you're wrong," he kidded. She didn't hear a word he said. Apparently her muse was a very loud voice inside her head. "I charge ten thousand dollars an hour. Twice that for modeling nude," he went on.

"Mmmm-hmm." She closed one eye and angled her head so far over he feared it might snap off. "Excellent."

He watched her sober concentration speculatively. It seemed Mona felt her importance as an artist transcended all else, and that modeling for her was a privilege any right-thinking human would do for no other reason than the heady joy of being glorified through her genius.

"A contrast in textures…" she said, preoccupied with her vision. She wagged a hand vaguely off to her left. "Lean against that tree and do something interesting with your arms."

He hesitated for a second, wondering what the hell she might think "something interesting" with his arms would be. Going to the tree, he slouched against it, crossed his ankles and slipped his hands inside his pockets. Not so much interesting as comfortable. He looked at the lake, smooth as glass. Not a breath of wind stirred the air. With the high humidity, it felt hotter than a firestorm in Hades, even in the shade.

"Marvelous. I love the sheen of sweat on your chest. Keep doing that."

He glanced her way. Hell, it was so hot, not "doing that" could cause heat stroke. "Sweat costs extra," he joked. When he got no reaction, he asked louder, "Arms interesting enough?"

"Beautiful."

He fought a grin. At least he had the approval of one of the local females. Getting too cocky might not be a good idea, though, since her absorption in his so-called beauty was plainly academic. All in all, his ability to charm the women of the Blue Moon Inn had been far from a stunning success, a relatively unfamiliar experience in his life. Women were usually putty in his hands. He leaned his head back against the rough bark and glanced up through the tree branches at flashes of the bright, cloudless sky.

"Ah, keep your head up," Mona said. "You have a great neck."

He closed his eyes, feeling weary.

"Yes, I like that," Mona said. "Your expression is poignantly joyless. There's nothing more aesthetically stimulating than a beautiful, sad man."

Her comment jolted him. Had he allowed his self-doubt to show? Even worse, had he actually allowed self-doubt to niggle at him? Cyborgs didn't doubt themselves. To get back on track mentally, he attempted a joke. "A sad, sweaty man is aesthetically stimulating?"

Mona seemed to come out of her artistic daze, and looked at him as though she actually heard his question. After a moment, she said solemnly, "Unquestionably. Like babies. It's an internal thing, a gut feeling that churns the emotions."

He had a bad moment when she mentioned the word "babies," a flashback to his own infant son surged to the forefront of his mind. A beloved child, so briefly on this earth. He still mourned.

"Aesthetic stimulation is very like the artistic impulse. Both are hard to explain, because they are felt rather than reasoned." She rambled on unaware of his pain. He struggled to bury the agony of his loss and concentrate on her dry discourse. "Over the years I have learned that what my artistic impulses dictate, I must execute. I've found one is singularly unsuccessful when one tries to fight one's artistic impulses."

He frowned, pondering her observation. She had a point. After a moment, he muttered, "That goes for other impulses, too."

"Say again?"

He shook his head and looked up, returning to the requested pose. "Never mind." He closed his eyes, trying not to think.

"Standing still for a long time is tiring," she said. "We'll take a break in fifteen minutes. Can you hold that grim expression until then?"

"No problem." A heavy dullness settled in his chest. The way he felt now, he could hold it forever. Time passed. Roth didn't know how much. He worked at blanking his mind. Maybe a second out of every minute it worked.

"Well, Mona, how's it going   Oh."

Roth's eyes snapped open as Hannah emerged from behind the stone wall. When her eyes met his, she came to an abrupt halt. She must have been picking wildflowers. Her arms were filled with them. Against his will, he couldn't help but admire her, standing there like a startled doe in that pink sundress, her hair pulled back in a low ponytail. Tendrils of the bright gold stuff crowned her head in an airy halo.

She loosely clutched her bouquet of bright yellows and baby blues, with a smattering of white and purple mixed in. Roth thought she looked like a blossom, too, a rare, pink rose with a gleaming gilt heart. This lovely, natural beauty stood so still, clearly startled to see Mona painting Roth and his naked chest. Silence stretched out between them. Mona's preoccupation with her artistic mission so consumed her she didn't notice

Hannah. Unsure why, Roth felt a need to respond. "She's doing a torso study."

"Mmm." Hannah blinked, looked down at the ground and took a step backward. It was obvious that she didn't want to speak to him, or even see him. Did she plan to back up until she was out of sight on the far side of the wall? Her conspicuous disquiet at running into him grated on his nerves, but he swallowed his annoyance and grinned. "I don't think she heard you."

"It's—I was only passing…" She gestured absently as though losing the rest of the thought.

"Passing—*by?*" he helped.

She looked confused. "What?"

"You were only passing *by?*"

"Oh—yes."

He angled his head to peer at Mona. "You have company," he said overly loud.

Mona jerked. "Uh…" Her concentrated expression changed to puzzlement. "Hmm? Did you say something, Mr. Jerric?"

"You have a visitor."

"It's not…" Hannah faltered, "I mean I was only passing."

"By," Roth added, unsure why. Maybe just for the connection. He balked at the thought.

"Don't go!" Mona said. "I've barely begun!"

He crooked a half grin. Mona's ability to concentrate was mammoth. He removed a hand from his pocket and indicated Hannah with an outstretched arm. "You have company."

"I was just passing—*by!*" Hannah moved to Mona's side and gave a cursory glance at the canvas. "You're working on something new?"

Mona sat back on her stool and admired her effort with a smile. "Yes. Inspiration struck. What do you think?"

Hannah took a closer look, her expression studious in a frowny way. Roth examined her face, her wrinkled nose. That nose wrinkle was quite stimulating, aesthetically and otherwise. He wondered what his chest had become in Mona's hands.

"Well?" Mona prodded. "Don't hold back."

Hannah nodded, and Roth sensed she took her time to form an answer. "It's, uh, definitely…a very…male chest."

"But is it aesthetically stimulating?" Roth asked, more interested in drawing her gaze than hearing her answer.

She faced him, giving him a full frontal eyeful of that wrinkled little nose. He enjoyed the view. She deliberated another beat before responding and cocked her chin up a notch. He knew whatever she planned to say would be anything but bland. "Mona has managed to turn your chest into something worth looking at."

For the second time in as many minutes he felt oddly like a sweepstakes winner. "The woman is a genius," he said. Due to a telltale twitch of his lips he couldn't wholly suppress his pleasure over their little dialog.

"Now, now, Hannah," Mona said. "I appreciate your compliment, naturally, but—" she looked first at her artwork, then she faced Roth " we must give credit where credit is due. Mr. Jerric has a superb torso." She nudged Hannah, drawing the younger woman's glance. "I've had a brilliant stroke. Go over there and stick a flower in a belt loop." She pointed at the bouquet. "That yellow daisy. The perfect soft contrast to his hard, male belly."

Hannah's expression went from disdainful to stricken. Roth ground his teeth. She hated the very idea and that annoyed the fire out of him. "Come on," he said, trying to appear nonchalant. "I won't bite."

She gave him a look that said a great deal.

"I won't kiss you, either, if that's what you're afraid of."

"Well, of course he won't. What an odd thing to say." Mona nudged Hannah again, since she was frozen to the spot. "Hurry, dear. There's only so much good light left."

"Okay. All right." Hannah said, moving haltingly toward Roth. She kept her eyes on her bouquet as she separated one yellow daisy from the rest of the flowers.

Roth watched her cheeks turn crimson. She no more wanted to stick a daisy in his belt than she wanted to work for him. As he witnessed her affliction he grew more and more annoyed. When she reached him, she spent as little time as possible sticking the stem of the flower into the belt loop nearest his belt buckle. "Is this okay?" she asked, already backing away.

Mona frowned critically. "A little straighter." She motioned with her hand. "Less horizontal. More vertical."

Roth watched her as she tentatively readjusted the flower according to Mona's directions. "Like this?" she asked, avoiding looking at Roth.

"That's better," Mona said. "A little straighter."

Roth watched Hannah, her cheeks so pink now he worried that she might be overheated.

"Are you okay?" he asked. "You look flushed."

She swallowed, met his gaze for the barest instant. "I'm fine," she said brusquely, quickly turning her back. "Look, Mona, I have to go—get these in water. And—and I'm not feeling too well."

Mona looked a little put out, but waved her off. "Well, go then." She pushed up from her stool and walked over to Roth. "I think maybe it would be best if I press it to your stomach. It'll stick to your sweat." She pressed on the flower. "There," she said with a satisfied nod. "It's perfect."

Roth watched Hannah go out of the corner of his eye. "I'm glad my sweat could help."

When she sat back down, she checked her wristwatch. "Rats and toads, Roth. It's nearly six-thirty. I need to clean my supplies and bathe before supper." She sighed and shook her head. "Why didn't you tell me we went way past time for your break?"

He shrugged. "Time flies when you're having fun."

Mona smiled, buying the lie. "So true, and you're a dream of a model."

"Flatterer." He could hear the strain in his voice and wondered if she could.

Mona stood and stretched. "No, no, no. I never flatter. You were perfection." Gathering up her brushes, she glanced at him. "You're excused." Her tone and bearing held a condescending note. The hippie prima donna had spoken.

He nodded. "Thanks."

"Can you pose for me tomorrow?"

He would rather be devoured by ravenous wolves. "We'll see," he said, too burdened by restlessness to concoct a good excuse not to. Recalling Hannah's conspicuous reluctance to be near him, he lowered himself into a squat beneath the tree. "I'll hang around for a while."

"Yes, you relax. You deserve to." She indicated the easel and canvas. "Would you mind carrying these to the house when you go back?"

"No problem." He removed the daisy. Focusing on the placid lake, he resisted the urge to stare at Hannah's backside as she swayed tauntingly away from him.

Mona went down the slope after Hannah. He knew this because his attention had veered immediately back to a certain titillating tush. He rested his elbows on his raised knees, absently fingering the flower, its stem, its petals, so soft and delicate. He ran it beneath his nose and sniffed. He thought he could detect her scent, but knew it was probably his imagination. He just wanted it so much he conjured it up in his head.

For a long time he sat there and stared at the flower, wanting to toss it away but not quite able to let it go.

CHAPTER ELEVEN

HUNKERED beneath that tree Roth underwent a brutal session of self-reflection and self-recrimination. This trip had been tough on him, teaching him a hard-earned lesson. No matter how he struggled, he couldn't totally leave his humanity behind. He had feelings, and from the day he'd come to the inn they'd battered at him, finally knocking out a chunk of his protective barrier. A surprisingly good thing came from it, though. The bloody, jagged hole the battering created allowed in some enlightenment.

He finally faced what he had known deep inside all along, but refused to see. He would never raze Joan's quaint old house to create a generic resort of concrete, glass and steel. His inability to convince the proprietress to step obediently into line didn't seem outrageous now that he saw everything with enlightened eyes.

Looking back, he realized his heart couldn't have been in the project, or steamrolling Joan would have been easy. Ever since he sold his high school physics teacher on the notion that a pop quiz had been unfair to the football squad he captained because of a championship game that interfered with studying—something even he couldn't swallow—he'd found he could talk almost anybody into anything.

So the truth was, he didn't really want to condemn these cool, pristine woodlands to make room for acres of sunbaked parking lots. Neither did he really want to demolish the moss-covered church ruins and surrounding wildflower gardens and replace them with stark, high-rise condos.

To do so would be a mistake. No matter how unfeeling he tried to become, he admitted if only to himself, he cared about the old place. The secluded, idyllic setting was valuable, true. But now he understood its real value couldn't be calculated in dollars and cents—not things like charm, character, tradition—or memories. Just as it stood, dusty, creaking plumbing and all, the inn was one of a small number of vanishing treasures, places of solace for the mind, body and soul. Uncorrupted and noble of spirit.

His resort fantasy had been a much needed mental sabbatical from the day-to-day reality of his work. Enjoyable for a time, but a fantasy nonetheless. He was the CEO of Jerric Oil, employing hundreds of people. He ran a successful corporation, built with his own hands. Why shouldn't he be proud of creating that?

This interlude at the Blue Moon Inn allowed him to see his life choices clearly and to understand what needed to change. What he told Hannah out in the lake came back to him—*a competent person knows when to ask for help*. Why should he work himself to death? Jerric Oil thrived. Why not delegate more responsibility to his capable vice presidents, relieving some of the pressure and stress in his life? Why didn't he deserve more than one vacation every five years? He deserved a life, too.

But what was his life to be? What would he do with the time he carved out for himself? Maybe he could travel, or take up a hobby. There were any number of enjoyable ways to fill his time. Stepping back from his busy life, indulging in this introspective detour had done its work. Now, he could get back to his.

He stood up, still holding the flower. He looked at it for another long minute, then tossed it onto the grass. Lifting his shirt off the nearby branch, he slung it over his shoulders like a towel, turned away, then turned back. Feeling like an idiot, he bent and retrieved the daisy and stuffed it in his pocket. Trying not to think about why he'd done such an irrational thing, he grabbed Mona's easel and the canvas of his torso. He took a long, close look at it. Other than the fact that the contours of his body were basically green, with touches of purple and yellow, it did look like a male chest. He trekked toward the house. On his way, he came to a decision. The day had come for him to put the Blue Moon Inn—and everyone in it—behind him.

He entered through the kitchen door to find Joan pulling a peach pie out of the oven. The place smelled like a happy home, if smells could create emotions. Of course they could, or the perfume business wouldn't be a multibillion-dollar industry.

Joan heard the screen door close and turned to see Roth enter and deposit Mona's canvas and easel in a corner. His hostess set the pie on a metal trivet on the kitchen table and pulled off her oven mitts. "Dinner will be in fifteen minutes, Ross."

He smiled, feeling spent, but determined. "I won't be at dinner. It's time for me to go."

Joan looked confused. "Not for two more days."

He grasped the dangling ends of his shirt and shrugged. "I need to get back." He inhaled the fragrant pie along with the mixed smells of bacon, onions and green pepper in a potato casserole steaming on the counter. Not to mention the delectable aroma of her apple-stuffed pork chops. If he ate much more of Joan's cooking he would need to spend two hours a day in the gym instead of one.

"At least stay for supper."

He shook his head. "I don't think so." His mind's eye pictured Hannah. He would do himself a favor by making a clean break. The last time he saw her he didn't know it would be his last. If he let himself see her again, knowing it, he might…what? He shook off visions of taking her in his arms and finished his thought with as little emotional involvement as possible. If he let himself see her again he might…weaken in some way.

It shook him to think about what way that might be. Hadn't he already asked her to come back to work for him? That went over well, *if* you liked being called insane. No, it was best this way—a clean, final break. He touched Joan's shoulder. "It's been a nice vacation."

She didn't look like she believed him. Or was it that she didn't agree. Why should she? He had caused her a great deal of anxiety. He toyed with the idea of relieving her mind about his change of heart. "Joan, I…" He stopped himself. No, let Hannah sink or swim. He would be interested in seeing how much good her efforts would actually do.

If she succeeded, then brava for her. If she failed and couldn't turn a profit before the back taxes and penalties were due, then he would buy the property and make it a gift to Joan. It was only right and fitting. Staying here had allowed him to become more in tune with his place in the world.

Besides, he knew what would happen if he offered Joan a loan to give her enterprise a jump-start toward getting out of the red. Hannah was so stubborn, proud and antagonistic toward anything tainted with the Jerric name, she would reject it categorically. She intended to prove her worth, come hell or high water. A loan from Roth Jerric would be like trying to douse a fire with gasoline.

If proving her self-worth was the visceral spark igniting her decision to take on the inn's financial crisis, she certainly had her chance. If she could make the inn profitable, she was a damn site more savvy than most financial managers. If she succeeded, he promised himself he would tell her exactly that.

Are you nuts, Jerric? he demanded silently. *You see the woman again and you're in trouble. You know it. Leave it be.* He was attracted to Hannah, dangerously so. Arm candy he could handle, but intimacy with a woman more involved than mere sex, no. Hannah didn't intend to be any man's "arm candy." Everything about her made that clear.

Though he felt—something—he decided to call "discontentment" over leaving her, it was time to go back and do what he was good at. In personal relationships he was criminally incompetent. *Go back to Oklahoma City. Put everything you and Hannah shared into a mental crypt, lock it and bury it deep. To be able to love you need to feel deeply enough to cry, and you don't. Not anymore.*

"What?" Joan asked, drawing him back. "What were you going to say?"

He shook his head. "Nothing. Never mind. I need to go."

"But you adore my apple-stuffed pork chops," Joan said.

He focused on her face, feeling actual regret. "Yes, I love your cooking. But business demands…" He let the sentence die and squeezed her shoulder. It was an odd thought, but he decided he might even miss being called "Ross Johnson" by this earnest little woman. "You understand," he added with an expressive nod, as though it needed no further explanation. The universal excuse, "business demands"—vague with consequential overtones—never failed, whether used as he rolled out of a woman's bed, or escaping the allure of a fetching spitfire he dare not see again, for fear of crawling back into her arms.

Hannah stared at the bouquet she'd arranged from the flowers gathered in the wildflower garden. It was beautiful, if she did say so herself. She had a knack for arranging flowers and decided such little niceties would become part of her job. If she and Joan were going to make a success of this place, things like fresh flowers could make big differences for no additional expense.

She checked her watch. "Oh, dear." It was ten minutes after seven. Why had nobody called her to supper? She pushed up from the edge of her bed and smoothed her pink sundress. She hadn't worn it since last summer and she'd forgotten how much she liked it, with its corset-style bodice, short, tiered skirt and ribbon detailing. It was more frivolous than most of her clothes, but its feminine, flowy style appealed to her...*and,* an imp in her head whispered, *it appealed to Roth, too, if that kiss in the kitchen was any indication.*

She felt both embarrassed and waywardly exhilarated by the memory. She laid her hands against her cheeks. Her fingers were icy in comparison to her blazing face. "Don't think about him," she cautioned. "Don't dwell on it." Roth Jerric wasn't worthy of heated emotions.

She grabbed the vase and left her room. Luscious scents wafted up from below, but she had no appetite for food. She wished her stomach wasn't tied in knots. Sitting next to Roth at the supper table would do nothing to calm her nerves.

She headed down the stairs, her nonchalant attitude all show. The last thing she planned to do was advertise how intensely Roth's stormy, stolen kiss affected her. She didn't want it to, but she couldn't deny that it did. That kiss was so hot and wild, she had almost jumped him out there modeling for Mona. Sticking that flower in his belt had been very nearly too much of a temptation to conquer. But she'd made it through, and she would make it through dinner. She had to.

With the determination of a warrior heading into battle, she put on a brave face and called out, "Sorry I'm late, but I wanted to get these flowers perfect." She rounded the corner into the dining room, a fake smile on her face. Fearing eye to eye contact with Roth, she stared at her bouquet. "How do you like them?"

"They're charming," Joan said.

"If I were into painting still life, I would commit them to canvas," Mona added.

Hannah winced at Mona's reminder that she wasn't into still-life painting. On the contrary, her current artistic bent ran to virile, half-naked men. Silence fell and stretched out. Not that Hannah expected Roth to comment, but she hoped he might.

Why must she crave a word of praise from him? Unable to help herself, she shifted her focus to his place at the table.

It was empty.

Any evidence that he was simply running late was also absent. No plate or utensils were set there. Hannah experienced a moment of disorientation that evolved quickly into a disturbing awareness. "Roth is gone," she whispered. A suffocating sensation of loss cut off her breath.

"Something came up with business." Joan lifted her coffee mug to her lips, then frowned in question. "Didn't he say goodbye?"

Hannah shook her head. Somewhere inside her heart a light went out. Forever. At that moment, she knew she would never again feel quite happy. The insight made no sense. She didn't want to care for Roth Jerric. Even so, that sad, undeniable truth blasted into her consciousness like an erupting volcano. It burned, the pain excruciating.

She cared—too much.

Roth was far from perfect, far from the sort of man she wanted to love—like Deacon Vance, an upright, caring human being if ever there was one. Still, no matter how hard she tried to convince her heart, one simple certainty remained—she had fallen desperately and illogically in love with Roth Jerric. A man unworthy of such a strong, breathless emotion. The knowledge twisted and turned her insides, and she choked down an errant sob.

A crashing sound jolted her from her bleak reverie. She realized the vase had slipped from her hands, shattering on the wood floor. *"Oh!"* She knelt and began to retrieve shards, as though quickly doing so would magically put the pieces back together. "Your lovely crystal vase," she cried. Her vision grew blurry and she wiped her eyes with the back of her hand.

Joan rose from her chair. "It's only a little broken glass and spilled water. That floor has seen worse." Hannah became aware that Joan knelt beside her. Dousing a cotton napkin in the puddle of water, she said, "Think nothing of it. We'll gather up these flowers and find another vase."

Hannah felt a cool hand on her chin, tilting her face toward her hostess. "Gracious, child—" Joan sounded bewildered "—it certainly isn't a tragedy worthy of tears."

Hannah wished with all her heart that was true.

CHAPTER TWELVE

HANNAH threw herself into saving the Blue Moon Inn using every inventive, inexpensive way she could think of to get the name and attributes of the place out to the public. She promoted it emphasizing its homey, old-fashioned character and stress-free solitude.

She used the Internet and Joan's chat room fellowships to attract guests. Her first attempt was to lure senior citizens craving "the good old days." To her amazement and gratification, enough of the sixty-plus set booked the inn to keep it full for three weeks solid. And entertaining them was easy. They spent time lolling on the lake bank dangling their feet in the water, taking quiet walks and playing cards on the porch. A Good Old Days picnic on the lawn was the hit of each week's outing, Joan's food always a crowd pleaser.

Next, Hannah went after nonconformist, nature freaks promoting Nature Lovers Weekends, and found a smattering of success there. Mona inspired another idea. Aimed at artsy-hippies, it was called Art Sharing Weekend. Would-be artists came and trumpeted their interpretation of art, be it flinging paint or mutating found objects into eclectic jewelry, bird feeders or dangling mobiles. In the evenings these artists discussed, critiqued and shared ideas over wine and cheese. In Hannah's opinion, some of the guests showed real talent. Some were certifiable. No matter, Mona was in her element.

Pie Weekend became a surprise hit and grew to six weekends in a row, after a larger than expected batch of young men and women signed up. Apparently, because many females involved in the women's lib movement of the 1960s and 1970s were too career-oriented to bother with cooking, a number of their offspring craved a return to traditional roles. That promotion proved to be an untapped marketing niche, a pleasant surprise, and one they jumped on.

Because of Joan's talent in the kitchen, their cookery promotions mushroomed in popularity. Their culinary weekends expanded, first into three-day weekends, then four-day retreats. After a few months, Hannah and Joan offered even lengthier promotions, such as Elite Entrees Week and Be A Genius With Grains Week.

Joan thrived on the attention as much as her pupils appreciated the down home atmosphere and old-fashioned, scratch cooking, a lost art in many families. Hannah felt a sense of pride, not only because of her efforts to give Joan the home she desperately wanted to keep, but because their attempts clearly enhanced the lives they touched.

Hannah worked an eighty-hour week the first several months. Besides her accounting duties and the drudgery of cleaning and cooking she shared with Joan, she needed to place a value on the inn, take into account its pluses and minuses, as well as the benefits reaped by paying guests. From this she calculated the cost to them and what they needed to charge—not exceeding what the market would bear, but enough that their financial situation benefited. That proved to be a delicate balancing act, changing with each promotion. It proved to be a difficult tightrope to walk, made more challenging because of Joan's overly generous nature. Still, little by little, small profits began to eat away at Joan's debt.

Hannah's tragically jumbled emotions over Roth were forced to take a back seat to the physical and mental strain of saving the Blue Moon Inn. Yet, deep in the night the truth tore its way through to the surface and kept her tossing and turning. Exhausted and teary, she fought against her hopeless love. Roth was wed to Jerric Oil and to the acquisition of the almighty dollar. He clearly cared nothing for her and had put her out of his thoughts the instant he left. Why must she cling to the memory of a man so undeserving?

Fighting her desire, she reminded herself, "He is a snake waiting under a rock for you to fail. And after you fall on your face, he plans to slither back and gobble up the leavings. How can you want him?" How could her heart be in such opposition to her brain? Day after day, night after night, month after month, her heart ached, but gave her no answer.

February began a cloudy, dreary month in more ways than mere weather. Not because the inn still floundered in debt, because it didn't. Somewhere in all those blurred days and months of finding ways to boost profits and pare losses, Joan's financial situation turned a corner. Sun finally began to shine on her bank account.

Hannah mailed the last check to pay off the inn's back taxes, plus penalties. All the guest rooms held paying clients, and Joan bustled around bubbly and full of vigor. They even managed to hire a local woman as day help, to do laundry and cleaning, allowing Joan and Hannah to concentrate on hostessing and managing.

But Hannah was blue. Even with the inn full of guests, she felt lonely and lost, failing miserably to banish Roth from her mind and heart. She didn't like to admit, even to herself, that the small town existence she had lived for the past seven months wasn't for her. She needed a bigger city, more people her own age. She loved the ballet and Broadway type theater, neither of which were available locally. She liked an occasional latte and a periodic rock concert from touring A-list musicians.

The beauty of Grand Lake, its tranquility, the small town intimacy held an appeal, too. But Hannah was restless. Lately she felt so confined and isolated she wanted to scream. Radiant sunsets and leisurely walks proved pathetically inadequate to blast Roth from her dreams.

So, a few weeks ago, she faced the truth. Her decision to become the inn's manager had been more emotionally motivated than judiciously considered. "Story of my life," she mumbled, aware that her recent past had taught her a great deal.

First, from her mother's plight, she learned the negatives of being too dependent on a man, which needed reinforcement, considering how she allowed Milo's egocentric control to sideline her good sense. She even learned a lesson from Roth, with his insight that nobody took Milo's opinion about women seriously. She experienced a crazy mix of annoyance and gratitude for his lesson—that she mustn't be so affected by every perceived slight that she flew off the handle before knowing all the facts. Clearly she was too emotional for her own good at times. She promised herself she would work on that.

Stretching, she scooted her chair back from her cramped, cubbyhole of a desk in the back bedroom she had shared with Joan the past half year. That was another reason she felt confined and hemmed in. She had no privacy.

Sharing the room became a necessity if they were to utilize the guest rooms wisely. Plus, on those occasions when Mona visited for the Art Sharing Weekends, her inflatable bed on their floor left hardly any room to maneuver, let alone work.

Chatting with a casual friend at the supermarket last week, quite by accident Hannah had found a potential day manager for the inn. Lucy Jones, a retired accountant, mentioned her desperation to get away from her husband's newfound love, the trombone. Or what she called "a motive for murder." Lucy's qualifications made her perfect manager material, plus she wanted out of her house so badly she would work for what they could afford to pay. A miracle in itself.

Not so accidentally, while surfing the Internet, Hannah found a small Income Tax Preparation firm in Tulsa that had recently lost its assistant manager. Already into tax season, the owner needed a qualified replacement, and fast. Hannah immediately faxed her résumé. That was this morning. Not an hour ago she got the job offer.

She had twenty-four hours to make up her mind. Setting aside her ballpoint, she stood up, her decision made. She would accept the offer. It wasn't like the job market was so great she could afford to hesitate. Plenty of other out-of-work accountants waited in the wings for the opportunity.

The small firm could potentially give her exactly what she was looking for. One day she could be manager, or maybe even buy out the owner. Plenty of future there for her to do exactly what she wanted with her career. A voice in her head added, *And Tulsa isn't where Roth Jerric lives.* Her mind trailed back along that well-trodden path. She recalled his acts of kindness when her silly heart soared with hope. But ultimately he remained a callous money-grubber. At least she could take satisfaction in the knowledge that he wouldn't be able to steal the Blue Moon Inn for pennies on the dollar.

Hopefully absence and distance would eventually help her forget him. *Just because it had failed to worked so far...* She shook herself, readjusted her thinking to a more positive plane. There was more to do in Tulsa to keep her mind occupied. "Like dating lots and lots of eligible men—nice, nonslithery, nonsnakelike men," she muttered.

Her vision blurred with misty doubt. Why did it seem so dark out there in her future? So forever-dark and empty? "No, no," she cried, fisting her hands. "It's a new day, a bright, shiny beginning." But she must act quickly. She sucked in a breath for courage. All that was left was breaking the news to Joan. Then, tomorrow she would go over the managerial duties with Lucy Jones. Afterward, in the evening, she would leave. It was best to get it done quickly. The pain would be over faster, like ripping off a bandage.

She felt sick to her stomach. Not because she thought her decision was wrong, but because she knew Joan would be terribly upset. The poor woman had no inkling Hannah planned to quit. Cowardice was to blame for that. The time never seemed right to bring it up. She knew Joan would be sad, and she hated to be the cause of sadness for someone she had grown to love.

In all honesty, she was sad, too. Joan was like family. Yet, even so, today was the day to turn the page in her life and move into the unknown. These past months she'd regained much of her self-confidence. She would do fine, though her heart would be slow to heal.

She was suddenly assailed by a terrible sense of despair. Who was she kidding? Her heart would never completely heal. She would carry the scars with her all the rest of her days. She choked off a sob and pressed her hands over her face. *Pull yourself together,* she berated inwardly. "Everybody carries around scars," she told herself, her voice rough. "End the pity party and get it over!"

With monumental effort, she held her head high and headed up the hallway toward the front of the inn. "Joan?" she called, surprised her voice sounded as normal as it did.

"I'm in the kitchen with my exotic cuisine class," Joan called out, a happy lilt in her tone.

Hannah checked her watch. She'd forgotten. Since the middle of January, Joan had held a class for locals on Wednesday afternoons, teaching them to prepare recipes she had picked up during her world travels with Dur.

"In Singapore," Joan was saying, "Dur and I loved beginning the day with a morning jog to a roadside stand to enjoy a breakfast of pork rib tea soup."

Hannah entered the kitchen to see Joan standing beside the stove where a large pot simmered. Three local women and one man sat at the kitchen table, set with placemats, napkins, bowls and spoons. Joan ladled soup from the steaming pot into a large, crockery bowl. "Say it for me. Bak Ku Teh."

The students repeated the name as Joan moved the serving dish to the table. "Excellent. Now, after our hard work, we shall have a savory taste of the mysterious orient." She filled the ladle and lifted one of the bowls. "In Singapore Bak Ku Teh is served with Chinese crullers for dunking and an extremely hardy black tea that we Americans might call the espresso of teas."

"What's a cruller?" asked Mrs. Brody, a petite, inquisitive octogenarian.

"It's a kind of bread," Joan said. "You can save a lot of time and energy by using frozen bread dough. Tear the thawed dough into pieces. Roll each piece between your hands until it's about the size of a small frankfurter. After the dough stands at room temperature for an hour, pull and twist the ends and deep fry."

"Gracious sakes alive, Joan, you know I can't eat fried foods," Mrs. Brody said.

Joan laughed. "Well, Aggie, it's not against the law to use dry toast for dipping."

The others laughed at Joan's joke.

Hannah smiled, but each second dragging by added a layer of tension to her overburdened nerves. While Joan served and chatted with her students, Hannah clutched her hands to keep from wringing them. After what seemed like an eternity, their hostess finally finished. "Joan," Hannah whispered, "I need to speak with you."

Joan looked up, a smile on her lips and a twinkle in her eyes. Hannah hated the knowledge that her announcement would extinguish both.

CHAPTER THIRTEEN

APRIL in Oklahoma gushed with new life. Yellow daffodils burst through the earth to herald the birth of spring. Redbud blossoms added a welcome blush to the greening landscape and white flowering dogwoods gladdened the shade of taller, sheltering trees.

The world seemed especially beautiful on this late April day as Roth turned down the bumpy drive toward the Blue Moon Inn, the familiar crunch of gravel beneath his tires loud through his open car windows. Joan's house came into view beyond a stand of greening oak trees.

He breathed deeply of the clean, lake-scented breeze, feeling energized—and nervous. Nearly a year separated him from the last time he had seen Hannah. Those months became a period of soul searching, making changes in his working life and his personal point of view.

After last summer's experiences at the inn, he went back to his firm and began to delegate authority, giving him time to live life outside his office. However, he found that more free time didn't necessarily mean a richer life. Gratuitous dating left him cold and empty. So he spent less time in pursuit of meaningless relationships and more of his days and nights in quiet reflection. After a great deal of self-examination, Roth saw that his avoidance of feeling deeply was nothing more than gutless insecurity.

His judgment might be faulty at times, but what human's wasn't? No matter how robotlike he had tried to become, it never brought him happiness or peace. Emotions like loss and grief were integral threads in the fabric of life. If he couldn't accept that, then he must come to terms with a life not truly lived.

He pulled to a stop on the gravel lot beside the inn, surprised to see three cars parked next to Joan's old sedan. Did the inn actually have guests? He smiled at the notion. Hadn't he known if anybody could get this place turned around, it would be Hannah? She had the grit and determination to do anything she put her mind to.

He stepped out of his car, feeling uneasy. What would she do when she saw him? They hadn't parted on the best of terms. Hell, they hadn't spent much time at all on good terms. She'd annoyed the fire out of him more often than not, but her memory refused to fade. From the night he left the inn last summer, her face, those eyes and the wild heat of her kisses haunted his dreams. Her memory stole into career achievements, leaving him restless and unfulfilled until finally, he let himself see the truth. His life *could* be complete—with Hannah.

He could be happy with her, decent, caring and uncalculating. With Hannah as his soul mate to share his joys and sorrows, he could let himself be human again. But stubborn, thickheaded cuss that he was, it took nine months to fully absorb how spineless he had been to close himself off. In the time it took to conceive and give birth, this truth gestated and grew inside him, at last allowing him to understand how much he needed, missed and—*loved* Hannah Hudson.

As he walked toward the inn a renewed wave of fear washed over him. What would she say to a marriage proposal? Being so twisted on the subject of her independence and a need to be singularly competent, would she allow the possibility of sharing her life with any man—much less him?

"You have a damn hard mission ahead of you, Jerric," he

muttered, climbing the porch steps. "The sales job of your life." So much rode on Hannah's heart. As he ascended, he felt like a condemned man mounting a scaffolding to face a hangman's noose. If she scoffed at his declaration of love, she condemned his heart to a breakneck plunge and a slow, suffocating death.

At the door, he stilled, momentarily paralyzed. Yet in spite of his crippling fear he experienced a rush of hot, unspeakable joy, knowing he would soon see her again. His chest felt as though it would burst. He exhaled, inhaled, pulling himself together. Nothing in his life had prepared him for this moment.

Where was the levelheaded, controlled Roth Jerric of Jerric Oil? He chuckled morosely. "You're in love, idiot." An irony hit him. He was okay with the misgiving gnawing at him, with his stomach clenched in a knot and the icy fear twisting around his heart, because it came with the territory of being fully alive. Human. He wanted that. Ever since the night under that crazy blue moon, knowing the bliss of being fully alive was all he wanted. It had just taken a while to figure it out.

With deepened resolve, he knocked.

As he waited, time slowed to a crawl. Would she answer the door? And if she did, would she smile with recognition? Or would those breathtaking eyes narrow and harden at the sight of him. Frigid dread shrouded him at the thought. Steeling himself, he shook it off. "Damn it, man. This is your life you're trying to resurrect. Don't fold up now."

When the door opened, and Joan appeared, he hid his disappointment with difficulty. "Hello." He smiled cordially. She looked the same, as did her aging dog, trailing inches behind her. He experienced a pleasant connection with the mutt and squatted on his haunches. "How are you, girl?" He held out a hand.

Missy Mis pitter-pattered up to him, allowing him to scratch her under the chin.

"It's been a while."

"Why, Ross Johnson!" Joan said, drawing his gaze. "This is a surprise."

He stood, taking her outstretched hand. "It's good to see you." He was startled to discover he felt an odd pleasure at being referred to as Ross Johnson again. Anxious to see Hannah, he swept the foyer with his gaze. An elderly couple ambled out of the dining room. Carrying steamy coffee mugs, they disappeared into the living room. So far, no Hannah. "It looks like you're doing a nice business these days."

"Oh, yes, very nice." She hesitated, worry dashing across her face for an instant before she masked it with her polite, proprietress expression. "The back taxes are paid, if that's your question. And I'm still not interested in selling."

The remark embarrassed him. How long ago had he forgotten about that fantasy. Meeting her resolute gaze, he smiled apologetically. "I didn't come here to bother you about that." He reflected for a moment on how selfish and single-minded he must have seemed to her. What an ass he was! "I apologize for—everything," he said. "I'm happy to hear you're doing well. I never doubted Hannah could do it."

"You didn't?"

He shook his head. "Not for a minute."

Her smile returned. "Well…that's news to me. I was under the impression you didn't like her."

He experienced a squeezing pain in his chest. He hadn't wanted to. He'd tried his damnedest not to. "On the contrary," he admitted. "I liked her from the beginning."

"You mean the night under the blue moon?"

His short burst of laughter held more self-consciousness than humor. "Yeah, I suppose." He remembered her beautiful eyes from before that night, but seeing her bathed in the light of the blue moon—that was the moment his life changed forever.

"Well, well…" Joan squeezed his hand with both of hers. "You're looking fit."

He wondered if she were being polite. The strain of the past nine months must show. "Do come in," she went on. "If you're here for a little vacation, you're in luck. Mr. and Mrs. Duckworth's first grandchild came into the world prematurely this morning. Naturally they scooted back to Joplin to see the baby. Their room is available until Friday."

"I see," he said, half listening. He would explode if he didn't see Hannah soon. "I'll think about it. Actually I'd like to see Hannah."

"Hannah?" Joan repeated.

She sounded bewildered. So much so he stopped searching the place with his eyes and returned his attention to her face. "Yes. Is she busy?"

Joan drew him inside. "Of course." She peered at her wristwatch. "People usually are on a workday, some even at six-thirty." She smiled at Roth. "She's a go-getter, that girl. I'm surprised a go-getter like yourself isn't still at work. What brings you here?"

Didn't he just tell her? He regarded her with searching gravity. "I came to speak to Hannah," he said distinctly. "I'd like to see her." He hoped that cleared up any confusion.

Joan's smile faded. "She's not here." She sighed and shook her head looking melancholy. "I was sorry to lose her as my manager, but a vibrant young woman like Hannah has a right to follow her heart."

He heard Joan's statement, but it didn't compute. "Follow her…" Disconcerted, he let the words trail off, a cold foreboding sweeping over him. A horrible thought struck. Had she married the sheriff? Was she another man's wife? Another man's love? Why the hell hadn't that probability entered his mind before now?

"Why, Ross, you look unwell." Joan tugged on his hand. "Come, sit. Have you eaten? Supper's over but there's plenty of spaghetti left."

He couldn't remember when he last ate and shook his head, more to purge the nightmare from his mind than to answer.

"Then you must eat something. How about a big piece of pecan pie?"

"Where?"

"Anywhere you want. Kitchen, dining room, or you could watch the bingo tournament in the living—"

"No," he interrupted, his vision still colored with the specter of Hannah as the bride of Deacon Vance. As bad as it was to imagine, he had to hear the truth. "Where is she?"

"Who?" Joan looked confused, her thoughts clearly on the best locale for feeding him pecan pie.

"Hannah." Roth pulled from Joan's hold and grasped her shoulders. "Where is Hannah?"

Joan's flinch told him his grip caused her pain and he dropped his hands. "Is she married?" he asked.

"Married?" Joan blinked. "You mean Hannah?"

Fear, stark and sharp made him want to howl like a wounded timber wolf, but somehow he managed to hold his crumbling control together. "Yes. Hannah. Did she marry the sheriff?"

"The sheriff?" Joan echoed, looking perplexed. "Why—no, whatever gave you that idea?"

He sucked in a breath, surprised to find he hadn't been breathing. "I thought…" His hope revived, he asked, "Where is she?"

"She's…" The older woman frowned, as though unsure what to say. "She moved away."

"But where?"

"She's still in Oklahoma, working at another job."

"When did she leave?"

"About a month ago," Joan said. "I miss her, but she's young and the lifestyle here was too pokey." She sighed heavily, almost theatrically. "I can understand how she felt. After all, when we were young Dur and I left to travel the world. Now of course, my priorities—"

"Yes, I'm aware of your priorities," Roth interrupted. "Where is she working?"

"Why?" Joan looked cautious.

"I need to see her," he said minimally, not a man to broadcast his private life or his intentions. Hannah should be the first to know of his feelings, his love.

Joan's expression grew guarded. "Why would you want to see her now, after all this time?"

He shook his head, frustrated. Why was he allowing this woman to interrogate him? "It's personal."

"Oh?" She tilted her head, staring at his expression, as though gauging his intentions.

"I don't want to upset her," he said, in an attempt at reassurance.

"Well…I don't know."

The strain of these past months had frayed his nerves to the breaking point. Exasperated, he pulled out his cell phone. "Never mind, I'll call information and get her number."

"I don't think they give out unlisted numbers, dear, but you could try."

He stilled, phone in hand.

She took the cell phone away and patted his arm. "Come. Have some pie and coffee. Mona's here. She'd love to see you. I have a chat room to visit for a few minutes. They count on me for a few comments about now." She took his arm and led him into the dining room, pressing him to sit. "Mona adores you," she chattered on, placing his cell on the table. "You couldn't know, but the painting of your torso was her first sale." Joan smiled. "I'll have her bring you a piece of pie. Fresh coffee's in the urn on the sideboard, as usual. Pour yourself a cup. When I get back from my chat room commitment, we'll talk. Perhaps then you can convince me why I should give you Hannah's telephone number and address."

Roth found himself seated at his former place at the dining

room table, cleared of all traces of supper. A new, white lace cloth covered the surface. A beige, crockery pitcher filled with an airy, wildflower bouquet served as a centerpiece. He sat forward, leaned heavily on his forearms and dropped his head to his hands. "I'm in Hell," he muttered. "Who knew there'd be lacy tablecloths and bouquets?"

Blackmail? Roth never thought a cherubic, elderly lady like Joan Peterson would resort to such underhanded tactics. But she had. He would get what he wanted only if he stayed the night. She promised to give him Hannah's location in the morning when he was "fresher." She said she couldn't in all good conscience send him on a "long drive" when he looked so "seedy." Funny how a man could look fit one minute and an hour later, after doing nothing more taxing than eat a piece of pecan pie, look too seedy to be allowed to drive.

So here he sat, in the Duckworth's abandoned room, in the dark and in agony, the information he needed held hostage by the whim of a sweet-little-old sadist. He hunched on the edge of the bed, elbows on his thighs, too tense and edgy to lie down. Why he'd even undressed he didn't know. In his state of mind, sleep didn't have a chance of giving him any peace. All he saw before him was a long, agonizing night of pacing or crouching on the edge of his bed, staring at the braided rug under his feet. Even that was a trial, since the rug was barely visible in the darkness.

"Blast it, Hannah," he mumbled between clenched teeth. "Where are you?"

A loud burst of noise brought his head up. Someone was knocking, and whoever it was sounded adamant. "Yes?"

"I don't care if you're decent or not, you oil-sucking SOB," came a female voice. "I'm coming in."

He knew that voice and his heart bounded over the moon. He jumped to his feet. His prayer had been answered. Hannah!

The fact that she called him an oil-sucking SOB did nothing to quell his new, buoyant mood.

The door burst open to disclose the most beautiful sight he could imagine. Backlit by hallway light, there she stood, as radiant as ever. Her blond hair glowed in splashy disarray around her face, spilling over her shoulders. She wore a body-hugging safari jacket, a pencil-thin skirt and precariously high heels. Add to that her sultry-stormy expression, and she could have walked right out of a slick fashion magazine.

She was so stunning, he wanted to cry. No, he wanted to laugh. Or shout. Maybe howl. Mostly he wanted to touch her, kiss her. He wanted to make love to her like he'd never made love to a woman before. And he wanted *her* to shout, howl, laugh, even shed a few tears—happy tears.

"Hi," he said, not caring that it was a lame, inadequate thing to say. Hell, standing there in navy boxer shorts, he'd already lost all hope of coming off like Prince Charming.

"Hi?" she demanded, stepping inside the room and slamming the door at her back. She was harder to see now, since the only light streamed in through the window from a three-quarter moon. "Is that all you have to say?"

"No." He grinned at her. He could almost feel her animosity, yet he couldn't help his happiness. "I have a lot to say."

"You bet you do." She stalked toward him, as angry as he'd ever seen her. "How dare you come back here, after all we've done to put this place in the black, and threaten to drill for oil on her property."

She was close now. Close enough for him to take in her scent. She smelled delicious. He could eat her up.

"How dare you buy up the drilling rights to Joan's property," she went on, poking him solidly in the chest to emphasize her point. "Coming in through a back door to steal her land. Drilling rigs will ruin her business. Nobody would want to stay here with filthy oil derricks and all the pipe and paraphernalia that goes with it. I've never heard such a sneaky, underhanded thing in my life."

He reached out and held her by the shoulders, gently but firmly. "It's good to see you, Hannah," he said. "You look wonderful."

Her glare mutated into a gape of shock. "What?"

He couldn't help himself and ran a finger from her cheek back over her ear, sweeping a strand of hair with it. So soft—the cheek, the hair. So tempting, he battled a reckless urge to pull her close and kiss her hard. "I said you look wonderful. I've missed you."

Her lips parted, so kissable. He could tell she wanted to say something but seemed to have a tough time coming up with the words. "I—you—I…" She shook herself, obviously trying to get back on track. Shoving on his chest, she stumbled backward out of his grasp. "Stop that! Doesn't the fact that I think you're a worm make any impression on you at all?"

"You don't really think I'm a worm," he offered more out of hope than belief.

"No, no," she said, her anger flaring. "You're right. I don't think you're a worm. Calling you a worm is an insult to worms. Honestly I can't think of anything base, cruel, foul and low enough to call you."

She was flawless, her body curvy and trim, as though nature had taken deliberate pains to carve her for the singular purpose of torturing him. He cleared a knot of longing from his throat. "Well, while you're thinking about it, let me ask you this," he said. "Who told you I owned the mineral rights to this property?"

"You're not denying that you do, are you?" she demanded.

He shook his head. "No. I do."

She glared. "So you admit you came here to rip Joan's heart out, informing her that if you couldn't steal her property one way, you'd found another way to do it."

He listened with troubled constraint. "Joan told you this?"

"When she called me tonight. Poor thing was hysterical."

"Really?" He hadn't seen any signs of hysteria. Only a stubborn refusal to give him Hannah's location, and her insistence that she would be negligent to send him off overtired. Hysterical? Hardly.

So, that cyber chat room thing she excused herself for had actually been the so-called "hysterical call." He gave Joan credit. She was as good an actress as she was vindictive. "Then you jumped in your car and drove here to be her knight in shining armor, to slay the Jerric dragon?"

Hannah swallowed, exhibiting a glimpse of the charming vulnerability she tried so desperately to hide. God, he loved her. He loved her strength, her loyalty. He even loved the way she struggled to conquer her fear and do the right thing. Resisting the aching need to take her in his arms was the hardest work he'd ever done.

"I had to do what I could," she said, "to make you see how horribly criminal it would be to drill. Cluttering this pristine land with oil equipment would ruin her livelihood, cripple the property's value and destroy its natural beauty. You'd be stealing her home as surely as you would if you'd bought it for its delinquent taxes."

She was right. Drilling for oil could blight the land around a drilling operation, though Jerric Oil never left land worse than they found it. Still, this wasn't the time for ecological debates. He scanned her face. The anguish in her eyes tugged at his heart. "I admire your passion," he said, unable to help himself. "As a matter of fact, I love your passion."

She blinked, looking uncertain. Angry, but uncertain. Obviously she hadn't expected him to say anything like that. "Excuse me?" she demanded, none too warmly.

She was a scrapper. You would have thought Joan was her baby chick. He could no longer fight his longing to hold her, and drew her into his arms. She came stiffly, but didn't protest, no doubt too shocked to react. "This may come as a horrible blow, Hannah," he murmured against her temple. "But I also love your loyalty, your courage and your tenacity. I've even fallen for your hotheaded impetuousness, because without it, you wouldn't be here now."

She pressed her hands against his chest but didn't shove. He loved the cool feel of her palms on his skin. Even if she was preparing to reject him, she didn't. Not yet. She merely lay her hands against his flesh. So far, so good. She lifted her face to better see his. "I—I don't understand," she whispered.

He brushed her forehead with his lips, unable to resist a small taste. "I'm saying I came here today to find you. But you were gone."

She stared, clearly in disbelief. "Find me?"

"Yes." He inhaled her fragrant hair.

"But the drilling…"

"I don't know how Joan found out I own the mineral rights, or whether she even knows, and just made it up. I never mentioned it to her. To be honest, I've owned the rights since my father passed away. He left them to my sister and me equally." She watched him searchingly as he spoke. "I could have drilled here for years, but I've never had any intention of drilling on this land. First, neither my sister nor I need the money." He smiled wanly. "More importantly, I wouldn't now, even if I did need the money. I like Joan too much."

She stared for a long moment. He enjoyed every second, holding her against him, inhaling her, watching the emotion glistening in her eyes. "You—you never…?"

He shook his head. "No."

"And you came here to…"

"Find you. Yes."

She was beautiful when she was at a loss. "But—why?"

"Can't you guess?"

She frowned, looking disoriented, then shook her head.

"Just a little?" he teased softly. "Can't you feel my heart?"

She nodded.

"Well?"

She regarded him. After a silent moment her expression began to show signs of a growing improbability, as though a thought that she couldn't believe had struck. "No," she said, her voice a raw exhale.

His heart lurched. "I thought it would shock you." *Damn it,* he'd feared she wouldn't take the news well.

The tension between them grew palpable, throbbing in the air like an echo of his pounding heart. He felt suddenly weary, empty. A cold wind swept through the hollow corridors of his soul. She was truly horrified by the idea that he could be in love with her. He'd hoped, how he'd hoped—

"What exactly are you saying, Roth?" she asked, her tone not as frozen and hard as he might have expected. It occurred to him that she lingered in his arms. Why? "I want to be clear about the reason you came to find me," she went on. "What is it you thought would shock me?"

Ah, she wanted blood. Well, why not? Revenge, they say, is sweet. He hadn't actually spoken the words aloud. He supposed he had an obligation to step up and say them. *Blast it,* he meant them and *blast it,* he came here to say them. No matter how contemptuous she might be, she was right, the words needed to be said.

He wanted to tell her how he felt, even knowing she would bitterly reject his proposal. He had no intention of going cowardly into the dark unknown. Not any longer. He'd been a robot long enough.

"All right," he said, solemnly. Fearing it would be for the last time, he ran a loving hand along her face and through her hair. Then he slipped his hand down along the sweet curve of her back, holding her close. "I'm in love with you, Hannah," he whispered. "I think I've loved you from that moment in the garden, under the blue moon, but I wouldn't let myself see it."

He smiled bleakly. "You were a pain in the neck, but I kept coming back for more. I kept wanting you no matter how much you loathed me and called me an SOB, I kept coming. Even after I left, hoping to forget you, I kept coming back to you in my head and my heart, until one day I realized I didn't want to live inside a block of ice any longer, with no human contact or feelings. I didn't want to be a numb SOB any longer. I wanted to be a man, a whole man.

"It took me a while to understand, but I finally do. And because I do, I want you to be my wife, my other half, my life." His voice broke and he felt foolish, looked away. In another second he'd be a blubbering fool. God, love could be humbling. "That's why I came," he said, his voice rough with emotion. "To find you and tell you what was in my heart."

She didn't say anything. Didn't move. Humbled and hurting but craving the sight of her, he made himself look into her face, gaze into her eyes, fearing what he might see.

He thought he caught a glimmer of something—what had it been?—behind her thunderstruck facade. His looked closer, prayed harder. Something stirred in those beautiful, expressive depths, something he would have thought impossible a moment ago.

"You love me?" she asked.

"More than life," he admitted softly.

Her expression serious, she studied him, looking perplexed. Every ticking second that passed grew more painful for Roth than the last. Yet, he refused to put up any pretense. No masks now. No false fronts. He waited, watched, the truth of his love written in his features, glittering in his eyes. An iron fist squeezed his chest and his breath came hard as he prepared himself for her disdainful laugh and bitter rejection.

Her hands began to slip upward along his chest. Now it was

his turn to be confused, uncertain. Her hands continued to slide over his flesh, across his shoulders to encircle his neck. "So, if you love me," she said, "what do you intend to do about it—I mean *besides* tell me?" She lifted her chin. "Are you all talk, Mr. Jerric?"

Her reaction stunned him. Thrilled would be a pale term for the wild, rampant exhilaration he felt. He opened his mouth, but no words came. Astounded but happier than he could ever remember being, he managed an awed smile.

"Well?" she asked, her lips quirking in a wily little smirk. "I'm waiting."

Glorious, shuddering happiness sprang up in his heart. No disdainful laughter. No bitter rejection. God was in his heaven, and He had truly heard his prayers. Beholden and humbled, he crushed her to him with trembling arms. "Darling, darling Hannah—my love," he said, his voice husky. "Will you marry me?"

She cocked her head and pursed her lips, as though in consideration. "I'll think about it."

He frowned, but it was all show. His heart soared into hyperspace. He was a man, reborn. "I'll give you five seconds to decide," he teased.

She arched an eyebrow at him. "Oh? Then what?"

He laughed softly, glorying in her smile, the dazzle of her sparkling eyes. "Then I'll give you five more, sweetheart."

She nodded. "As long as we understand each other." She brushed his jaw with her lips. "Then my answer is yes. Now, kiss me."

It amazed him how quickly a botched life could turn around and become a paradise on earth. Hannah's "yes" breathed life into an empty hulk and gave him back his humanity. "You'd kiss an oil-sucking SOB?"

"Never met one," she whispered, nibbling seductively. "Now, pretty man, take off your pants."

He chuckled deep in his chest. Euphoric and still not quite believing his good fortune, he lifted her into his arms. "I'm a sucker for flowery speeches." He settled her on the bed and sat down, leaning over her. The shock of learning of her love began to wear off. Resting an arm on the other side of her body, he smiled down at her. "I thought you hated me."

"I tried, darling," she murmured. "With all my heart, I tried." She took his face between her hands. "You see, I fell in love with you the day I met you at Jerric Oil. Milo was a pale substitute. I see that now." She sighed and shook her head at the recollection. "When I thought you said I was mediocre, you broke my heart. I quit my job because I couldn't bear to be around you—"

"But I didn't—"

"I know, I know," she interrupted. "But by the time I found out, the man my heart wanted you to be wasn't the man you were—so hard and cold-blooded, trying to take Joan's home."

He felt the sting of truth in her words. "I was wrong. I realized that. I almost offered Joan a loan."

She bit her lip, wide-eyed with surprise. "Really?"

"Yes, but I knew you would never agree."

She smiled, but her eyes showed the anguish of memories. "You were right. I was so angry with you, so disappointed that my heart could want a man so—" Her voice broke and she cleared her throat. "I think I worked twice as hard to prove myself competent because I was so broken up, so lost, so furious with both you and myself." A melancholy laugh escaped her throat. "My fury and disillusionment for you got me through— probably helped me get the inn in the black."

He shook his head at the irony. "I'm sorry for being such a bastard."

She pressed a finger lightly against his lips. "Hush, darling. I'm saying you did me a favor. I got my self-esteem back and Joan kept her home."

"I knew you'd succeed," he said. "I've never met a woman so obviously and completely—well, for lack of a better word—perfect."

She lifted her hand and brushed her thumb beneath his eye. He became aware that he'd shed a tear. "And you, Roth Jerric, turned out to be the man my heart knew you were." She drew him down, caressing his lips with hers. "I'm so in love with you, I can't even begin to tell you."

His heart too full for words, he settled his mouth over hers. Hannah's lips parted, encouraging him to fully possess her mouth. Lazily, sensuously his tongue teased, explored and thrust. She moaned with desire as their deep kiss made wordless promises, stirring embers, long tamped down, but quickly kindled to flame.

A wild surge of pleasure coursed through Roth. At long last he and his beloved Hannah could lay aside their doubts and fears, understanding that happiness—as life—came with no guarantees, only possibilities.

Such wonderful possibilities.

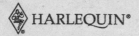

Coming Next Month

#3899 THE SHEIKH'S SECRET Barbara McMahon

Laura has been swept off her feet by a gorgeous new man—she's never felt so special! But as they become close, Talique is torn. Laura doesn't know his real name, his past, even that he is a sheikh! All she knows is the perfect world he has created for her. And just as his secret plan is about to be revealed, he realizes that his intentions have changed: he wants Laura as his bride!

#3900 THE HEIR'S CHOSEN BRIDE Marion Lennox
Castle at Dolphin Bay

As a widow and single mom, Susan is wary about meeting the man who has just inherited the rambling castle in Australia where she and her small daughter live. Surely New York financier Hamish Douglas will want to sell up? Hamish had planned to turn the castle into a luxury hotel, that is until he had met the beautiful Susie.

#3901 THEIR UNFINISHED BUSINESS Jackie Braun
The Conlans of Trillium Island

Even after ten years, Ali Conlan's heart still beats strongly for the man who had left without a goodbye—and her body still responded to his bad-boy confidence and winning smile. But she knew his visit was all about business: he was now a partner in her family's resort. Or was his return to Trillium about unfinished business of a different sort?

#3902 THE TYCOON'S PROPOSAL Leigh Michaels

With the holiday season approaching, Lissa Morgan is stuck without a job, and the roof over her head is only temporary! So when a live-in job is offered to her, Lissa snaps it up. What she doesn't realize is that she will be in close proximity to Kurt Callahan—the man who had broken her heart years before. Can Lissa forgive and forget?